COTTAGE
in the
VALE

THE AUTHOR Wilfred Pereira was born in London and educated at Wimbledon College. He trained as an aeronautical engineer and became an aviation writer. While researching his books on RAF Lyneham and Brize Norton he wrote *Cottage In The Country* by way of light relief. The experiences of the villagers of Severnham are now followed up in *Cottage in the Vale* which, like its successful predecessor, is based on his own experiences of country living. His interests are people, places and stories about them and both Cottage books happily combine all three.

Cover illustration: Detail taken from *A Gloucestershire Landscape* by John Limbrey MCSD (Private Collection)

Books by the same author

COTTAGE
in the
VALE

WILFRED PEREIRA

Line drawings by Ann Todd

THE WINDRUSH PRESS · GLOUCESTERSHIRE

First published in Great Britain in 1995
by The Windrush Press
Little Window, High Street,
Moreton-in-Marsh
Gloucestershire GL56 0LL

Telephone: 01608 652012
Fax: 01608 652125

British Library Cataloguing in Publication Data
A catalogue record for this book is available from
the British Library

ISBN 0 900075 09 0

Typeset by Archetype, Stow-on-the-Wold
Printed and bound in Great Britain by Biddles Ltd., Guildford

Contents

Author's Note

My Severnham is a synthesis of the villages along the Severn Vale. Likewise my characters are amalgams of many people met over the years and therefore fictitious. The aim is not to portray any known person, but to interest and amuse with my country tales.

Great Dame

It seems no time at all since I left London for a cottage in the country. I had become fed up with City working, suburban commuting and paying high prices for basic requirements. There were too many people, too much hassle. I needed more space and a simpler lifestyle. Thus, when the company wanted someone to open a Cheltenham branch office, I was the first to volunteer.

During the same period, I began searching for my country cottage. Eventually I found one in a great loop of the River Severn. The property was run down and needed renovation. There were no services such as electricity, water and drainage. While these were being installed, I discovered Severnham village and district was rich in characters and situations.

There were my neighbours Samuel and Evangeline Hopskip; the unlucky Grange across the lane; the Reverend Andrew Mead who preferred saving old cars to souls and his practical wife wrongly nicknamed Dottie; the local Twist and Fluke families maintaining their ancient grudge from the War of the Roses.

Apart from the locals, there were also the many newcomers adding to an already rich mix. Nothing was quite what appeared on the surface at Severnham and I will begin with a typical yet somewhat strange story which I witnessed from the beginning to the end. It began early one morning after a particularly wet and stormy night.

The storm blew itself out in the early hours and by dawn the sky was innocent. I went downstairs to a garden littered with twigs and other debris. My neighbour, Samuel Hopskip, was already tidying up on his side of the hedge. He said, 'Fair old blow,' and we set about our respective tasks.

As we worked in silence, a milk lorry came along the lane and stopped nearby. A short stout man jumped down from the passenger side. He wore a shiny blue suit with a brown felt hat and suede shoes. The cheap suitcase he carried had seen better days. It was held together by a length of cord.

Samuel, a man of few words, now uttered four of them. I did not understand him at the time, but this is what he said,

'Sandy Porridge. Great Dame.'

We then watched the newcomer walk round the church bend in our lane and enter the vicarage.

An hour later, while I was having breakfast, I saw Dorothy Mead emerge from the vicarage and start walking towards my cottage. The vicar's wife – popularly known as Dottie – was one of my favourite people. She just looked dotty due to forever falling down hair, big granny glasses and weird assortments of clothes. Apart from those Dottie was a truly good person, a giver in life rather than a taker.

'I've come to ask you a favour,' she said.

'Granted,' I replied which made her laugh.

'But you don't know what it is. Yet.'

Dorothy Mead accepted a cup of coffee and explained. She had a problem concerning a Mr Porritt who arrived every year to help with the Severnham village children's pantomime. Normally people called Nicholson put him up, but this year they were bitten by the flu bug. Dottie asked if I could accommodate Porritt, adding he did not pay anything. I said,

'Bring him round when you like.'

Dottie brought Mr Porritt round mid-morning. At close quarters he looked like a friendly frog with a broad yet deferential grin. His blue suit was well worn and the shirt frayed at the collar and cuffs. Dottie said,

'Mr Porritt is very grateful.'

'It is most Christian of you, Sir,' he intoned.

'What should I call you?'

'Everyone calls me Sandy. Sandy Porridge. It was my stage name. When I truly trod the boards.'

'Well Sandy, let me show you your room.'

Leaving him in the spare bedroom, I went downstairs to Dottie who whispered,

'Thanks ever so. He won't be any trouble.'

'I'm sure.'

Cottage in the Vale

'Would you like some cash from the church fund?'

'Pleased to help. Let's leave it and see how things work out. Which I am certain they will.'

Thus Sandy Porridge arrived to stay a while with me.

Smiler the cat was interested, especially when the visitor showed him a little trick. Sandy took out a clean handkerchief, rolled and knotted it to resemble a mouse. He then began to stroke the bundle. Smiler watched intently. When Sandy caused the cloth mouse to jump, the cat easily caught it. However, after sniffing the rolled up handkerchief, Smiler turned and strolled out of the room.

'Wonderful creatures,' Sandy beamed.

'Indeed,' I nodded.

'Every theatre has one you know. To discourage mice in return for regular food and warmth. Different personalities, yet it is interesting how they all keep off the stage.'

'Why is that?'

'Stages are cold and draughty places. Audiences don't realise it. The actors may appear as if they are sunning themselves on the Riviera while trying not to shiver . . .'

I encouraged Sandy to talk and soon learned his life story. He had been born in a dressing room at the Theatre Royal, Nottingham; carried with his cradle round the northern circuits; played page boys and other children's parts from the age of two.

Sandy married an actress – long since dead – and had three sons who all went into the Services. They too married, but moved away from him. Since his retirement many years ago, he lived with 'The infamous Mrs Maynard at Cradley Heath.'

'Why infamous?' I wanted to know.

'Elsa Maynard was the most powerful Lady Macbeth ever seen. She never reached the West End, nor Stratford, but Elsa's interpretation made her famous – or rather infamous.'

'Why infamous?' I persisted.

'Well, *Macbeth* is an unlucky play. Whenever Elsa had anything to do with it, there was some accident or other. Macbeth would break a limb or Macduff be hit by a sword.'

'And you live with her now?'

'She runs a boarding house for old actors. It's big enough to take from ten to twelve guests. I have an attic room with a fine view of Cradley Heath.'

'That's nice,' I remarked, hastily adding, 'It must be interesting. All you ex-actors.'

'Not quite ex, we hope.'

'You must talk of old times.'

'Yes, yes,' he agreed. 'In the evenings we often have play readings. Elsa always wants to do her Lady Macbeth so we have to dissuade her.'

'Why?'

'Because of the accidents,' Sandy retorted. 'One or other of us usually pops off soon afterwards. She can then advertise there's a room to spare.'

'Ah! I see!' It conjured up an interesting picture of night life at Cradley Heath.

A meeting had been arranged in the church hall to plan the pantomime and I went along to see how Sandy would fare.

Here I should mention the church hall also serves as the school hall and village hall. Because the church owns the hall, Andy Mead our vicar uses the place to renovate old cars. For the rest of the year Severnham folks tend to put up with his eccentricity. However, as Christmas approaches, pressure is increased on Andy to clean up and clear out.

In all fairness, he does make a stab at both, but his efforts are not good enough for the village mums. So, from late November onwards, they become more ruthless. They begin by shoving everything lying about in the dustbin. Then they start emptying shelves and lockers of spanner sets and spare gaskets, tins of hydraulic fluid and touching-up paint.

Their housekeeping skills intensify as November turns to December when they wash down the woodwork, scrub the floors and set out the chairs, dusting each one as they go. They refuse to be diverted by Andy wandering among them asking if anyone has seen his tyre gauge or ratchet screwdriver.

Such was the scene when I slipped into the hall. At the back Andy, wearing his electric blue baseball cap with 'The Good News' emblazoned on it, was endeavouring to deflect the implacable working ladies. At the front children from the village school sat looking up at Dottie as she led Mr Porritt on to the bare stage.

'Children,' said Dottie, 'once again we are delighted to have Sandy Porridge with us. This year he has come to direct and act in another pantomime of his choice. Which will be . . . ' Dottie paused for the desired effect, '*Cinderella*.'

A ripple of appreciation ran through the infant ranks.

'Therefore, without wasting any more time,' Dottie stepped back, 'I'll leave Sandy to get on with it.'

Dottie left the stage and came to sit next to me.

'Watch this,' she murmured.

So far Sandy had not done or said anything. He simply

stood there grinning down at the children while they looked up at him. Eventually a little girl giggled. To my surprise Sandy imitated her giggle.

'He's an excellent mimic,' Dottie whispered.

The two opening giggles caused more. A boy make an awkward gesture and Sandy did the same. A girl squirmed with merriment and so did Sandy. Without saying a word he had them responding. In no time at all they were laughing at him and each other. It was a treat to watch their joint merriment.

'But we must be serious,' Sandy chided them before bursting into more giggles. 'Cinderella is a serious subject. Poor Cinders with her wicked mother-in-law and those awful sisters. You know how terrible sisters can be, don't you? Oh yes they are. Come on. Shout it out. Oh yes they are!'

'Oh yes they are!' the children shouted back.

For the next hour, I sat and watched fascinated. Sandy began by selecting the children to play in the pantomime. He chose the girl who had first giggled as Cinders. He then went on to allocate the other parts, making each sound vitally important, while reserving the role of the Great Dame for himself.

After that the children's mothers, who happened to be dusting nearby, were told of the outfits they would have to make for their offspring. Cinderella needed two – a dress of rags and a beautiful ballgown. Sandy went into great detail about the costumes, ensuring the mothers understood and agreed what was needed.

At the end of the first session, the indcfatigable mums produced tea and four kinds of cake. Sandy sat among his cast, Dottie helped the mothers and Andy Mead confided in me. He muttered,

'My feelers have disappeared.'

'Your what?'

'My best set of feeler gauges. No one has seen them.'

'I'm sure they'll turn up.' Which they did.

Later Sandy and I walked back to the cottage.

'Enthusiasm,' he stressed. 'One must capture enthusiasm. Everything else stems from it. When I was young – playing a page boy or a spear carrier – I would often become bored. That is until my parents told me how important the smallest part is. The play's the thing – as the Bard so correctly informed us.'

Mr Porritt could be called the perfect guest. As Dottie had told me, he was clean and quiet. He kept his room tidy, left the bathroom as he found it and appreciated all I did for him. In the evenings his preferences were to read if I was busy or to talk if I wished.

During his stay at the cottage he was reading *Tristram Shandy*, a book I found impenetrable. Porritt had it in a fine classic edition with a bookmark of soft green leather. He read slowly, very slowly, his lips often mouthing the conversations. At the end of a reading session, his forefinger would trace back a line or two as he committed the final words to memory.

One evening I asked him if he liked television.

'Not a lot,' he replied.

'Why not?'

'The acting is so poor.'

'Why is that?'

'They don't have to act at all. A raised eyebrow. A sideway glance. It's money for old rope. Also they don't get to see the sets until the last minute so they keep making silly mistakes.'

'Such as?'

8

'With their entrances and exits. Doors for example. Those on sets are flimsy. Seldom work properly. Watch television actors with doors. And another thing, when will they learn to hold a cup properly?'

Meanwhile rehearsals for the Christmas pantomime went well. Sandy and the children would have a daily session and within a week everyone entered into the spirit of the piece. The little girl playing Cinderella drooped when she was down and stood proudly as her wishes were fulfilled. Two boys had the parts of the wicked sisters and they were encouraged by Sandy to pull nasty faces and be thoroughly objectionable to Cinders.

At the same time the church hall was being transformed. Volunteers worked on the stage, building the sets required, ensuring the curtains and lights operated correctly. Others put up decorations in the foyer and auditorium, renovated the box office and changing rooms.

There were two changing rooms – the larger for the kids and a small one allocated to Sandy Porridge. He had the same room each year, but this time there were improvements – a wall mirror ringed by electric light bulbs, a shallow makeup shelf and a tiny wardrobe. It was the nearest he would ever get to the dressing rooms of his earlier career.

'I hope you like it,' said Dottie, who had redecorated the room herself.

'Excellent!' he assured her.

'What about your costumes?'

'They are coming to the cottage tomorrow. By special delivery.'

I was out on business the next day and did not return

home until late in the dark December afternoon. The front door light was on, also one in Sandy's room. I opened the door, put down the briefcase and was hanging up my coat when he called from the top of the stairs.

'Is that you?'

'That's me!' I called back.

'What do you think of this?'

I had temporarily forgotten about the pantomime so the sight which greeted me on the stairs proved all the more vivid. Sandy was wearing an enormous pink wig and a voluminous ball gown. The whole outfit had been designed to reflect the worst possible taste. There were buttons, bows and other accessories everywhere in a rainbow of colours.

'Good Lord!' I exclaimed.

'This is my first act outfit,' Sandy informed me. 'The one for the second is even more lurid.'

'Impossible.'

The other had been laid out on his bed. It was an assembly of acid greens together with a fluorescent orange wig.

'There's a lot of it,' I observed.

'Yes,' Sandy confirmed, 'and I've only twenty minutes to change between the two acts.'

'Rather you than me.'

'The kids'll love it,' he smiled happily.

The schedule for the pantomime ran as follows. There would be full rehearsals during the final week and a dress rehearsal on the afternoon before Christmas Eve. The dress rehearsal had become an invitation only occasion for the families and friends of those involved.

Following Christmas, the first official performance

was on the afternoon of Boxing Day. Two others were laid on aimed at Severnham folk and a further three for schoolchildren at Lower Severnham, Twiggleswood and Severnside Comprehensive. All in all, it was a demanding programme.

I went to the dress rehearsal and became caught up in the excitement. The children and their mothers were simultaneously apprehensive and high spirited. They tried to remember their lines while mothers dressed and fussed round them.

'Come on Sarah!'

'What have you done to your hair?'

'Stand up straight!'

'Careful or you'll rip that ball gown.'

In Sandy's small dressing room, he worked quietly and professionally. The shocking pink outfit was fitted, the exaggerated make-up applied, the high wig secured.

'How are the kids doing?' he asked when I looked in.

'Fine.'

'They'll be a bit nervous,' he grinned, 'but I'll chivvy them along.'

This is what he did. To the proud fathers and mothers, also to envious brothers and sisters, it looked as if the stage children were word perfect. In reality Sandy fed them their lines, controlled their timing and kept the whole pantomime moving on course.

He was an enthusiast for audience participation especially among the other children there. He called to them, harangued them and drew from them louder and louder responses of 'Oh yes he will!' or 'Oh no he won't!'

The Nicholsons, who normally put Sandy up and who had recovered from their bout of flu, sat at the back with me.

'Isn't Sandy wonderful?' said Mrs Nicholson, a catering officer.

'He certainly is.'

'I'm taking him to Cradley Heath,' said Mr Nicholson, an electrical contractor. 'This evening,' he added.

'And he's coming back to us after Christmas,' his wife made sure I understood what Dottie had already told me.

'Of course,' I said, 'though I shall miss him.'

After the dress rehearsal, everyone triumphantly talked at once. I slipped round to the small dressing room where Sandy was changing and the Nicholsons waiting.

'Great performance!' I said to him. 'You were all great.'

'Thanks,' he replied while detaching the huge orange wig. 'Thanks for having me.'

Christmas came with all its activities and festivities. There were services in our beautifully decorated church, a party at The Restoration Inn and another with the Spinks. Early on Boxing Day morning, I was in the garden when Mr Nicholson went past and waved. He had to collect Sandy from Cradley Heath and bring him for the afternoon performance.

My cottage is close to the church hall. I decided to drop in later and have a word with Sandy. Mrs Nicholson was by the door and she moved to intercept me.

'We got him here in time.'

'Great!'

'And gave him lunch.'

'Good for you.'

'He's not looking well.'

'Oh?'

12

'We think,' Mrs Nicholson remarked, 'he is sickening for something.'

'Perhaps he was carried away by the Christmas spirit,' I suggested.

'When we looked after him,' she said meaningfully, 'there was no trouble.'

'I hope he recovers soon.'

What Mrs Nicholson had implied annoyed me, yet she was right. Sandy did not look well. There were dark shadows under his eyes. His skin had a waxy look to it.

'How are you?' I asked him.

'Splendid, splendid.'

'You don't look it.'

'Some bug,' he admitted. 'But never fear. The show will go on.'

Which it did. The cast had benefited from the Christmas break and Sandy himself rose to the occasion. He was more vigorous, more preposterous than I had ever seen him. His audience became increasingly enthusiastic. The children in it chanted their responses with increasing vigour. It was a triumph and yet . . .

'Stupid woman,' Dottie said to me when we met next day.

'Who's a stupid woman?'

'Tessa Nicholson. She keeps telling everyone that Mr Porritt was never ill when he stayed at her house.'

'For goodness sake!' I said.

'That's what I told her,' Dottie emphasised. 'She's implying her cooking is perfect while yours . . . Or someone else's . . . '

'How silly. But Sandy doesn't look too good. Has he seen a doctor?'

13

'No,' Dottie said slowly. 'I suggested it to him and was put in my place. The show will go on, he assured me.'

'And me.'

'This could well be Sandy's last appearance in Severnham. I also learned he's eighty-four.'

Sandy proceeded to show everyone how professional he was. He put everything into the remaining shows – the other two for Severnham Village, the further three for Lower Severnham, Twiggleswood and Severnside Comprehensive. Before the curtain went up he looked ghastly and afterwards he was exhausted. We heard he slept through each morning at the Nicholsons. The worthy Tessa relayed his condition to all who would listen.

'If only I had looked after him to begin with.'

In the end it was a self-defeating argument because people looked elsewhere when they saw her coming.

Like most who knew Sandy's age and condition, I was concerned for him. I decided to go and see the second half of his last performance, then to say goodbye and wish him all the best. I arrived at the church hall as the curtain came down on the first act. The audience was happy and the sellers of ice creams busy, but Dottie looked concerned. She said to me,

'Sandy's been taken ill. Would you get Dr Prosser?'

Somehow I was not surprised. I ran out of the hall, cut across the village green and hurried up Restoration Lane. Dr Prosser, I should mention, is a fine practitioner though he does not take kindly to out-of-hours sickness.

'Yes, yes,' he said irritably, with a backward glance at the flickering television, 'I was warned about this by Mrs Nicholson.' Shrugging on an overcoat, he snatched up his bag and followed me.

14

Sandy's dressing room was at the far end of a narrow passage. The Nicholsons stood at the entrance to it, Dottie halfway along and Andy in the doorway hiding what lay beyond. Dr Prosser hurried past everyone and disappeared into the room. A long silence followed.

At last the doctor came out of the room shutting the door behind him.

'He's dead,' Prosser informed us.

'Dead,' Mrs Nicholson informed me.

Andy Mead asked,

'What do we do now?'

'The show can't go on,' said Dottie. 'You'll have to tell them. About poor Sandy.'

'Poor Mr Porritt,' Mrs Nicholson told me.

'Telephone?' asked Dr Prosser.

'I'll show you,' Dottie said. She turned to her husband. 'Go on Andy. The sooner the better.'

'How shall I put it?' Andy seemed dazed.

'Simply,' Dottie replied. 'No sermons.'

'No sermons,' Mrs Nicholson repeated. I could have slapped her. Noticing the tension, Mr Nicholson said,

'Come on my dear. There's nothing more we can do here.'

'There isn't,' Tessa agreed and swept out of the building. Still looking dazed Andy came towards me. He lurched past and went through the double swing doors into the auditorium.

I decided to stand outside the dressing room door in case anyone inadvertently came to visit Sandy. No sooner had I taken up position than PC Stan Oakshott appeared. He was a good solid man to have in a crisis.

'Mrs Mead,' Stan said, 'asked me to guard this door.'

'Ah yes.'

'She'd like you to make sure the vicar's all right.'

'Ah.'

I went into the auditorium wondering how Dottie acquired her nickname. She certainly kept a cool head.

The audience was beginning to grow restless as Andy Mead climbed on the stage and moved along in front of the curtain. Silence fell when he raised his hands.

'Dearly beloved . . . er, ladies and gentlemen. Also boys and girls. I have a sad announcement to make. Sandy Porridge – I mean Mr Porritt – is not well . . . ' Andy stopped and the audience waited. 'In fact, I have to tell you, Sandy passed away during the interval.'

No one made a move or uttered a sound.

'In the circumstances,' Andy struggled on, 'tonight's show has ended.' He paused once more. 'I am sorry boys and girls, but Sandy won't be here to entertain you any more.'

There was a short shocked silence until several little voices piped up hopefully,

'Oh yes he will.'

Afterwards there was the funeral. I travelled to Cradley Heath with the Meads in their renovated but still rusting old car. The Nicholsons went as well. In a recent registration BMW.

The crematorium was empty but for the staff.

'Oh yes,' one of them confirmed. 'Porritt's the first.'

So we stood around awkwardly with the Nicholsons. Tessa stared into the distance. Her husband thought there might be snow later.

Eventually a minibus arrived at the crematorium. It contained nine elderly men and one statuesque woman. The men, although short and tall, fat and thin, all had the look of Sandy about them. The appearance of actors. They were alert, stood well and showed a sense of grouping.

The woman who drove the bus wore a floppy cap, long coat, gauntlet gloves and high boots of black leather. She possessed clean cut features, a commanding eye, a ringing voice.

'Elsa Maynard.' The fingertips of the gloves were briefly extended to us in turn.

'Usually,' said Mrs Nicholson, 'I look after Mr Porritt. But this year we had flu, you understand?'

'He had a good innings . . . ' Mr Nicholson began.

'That's not the point,' Tessa informed him and us.

'We've got the point . . . ' Dottie muttered, then Andy cut in by announcing,

'I think they want us inside.'

When we were outside again, Mrs Nicholson had to make her point once more. She said to Elsa,

'I do hope another of your gentlemen actor friends will come to Severnham next Christmas and help us with our little show. Whoever it is, I promise to look after him personally.'

Mrs Maynard did not appear to hear her. Instead Elsa said,

'We must be going. Neville's chest is playing up and Tristan has to see a specialist this morning.'

The 'gentlemen actor friends' smiled and nodded as Elsa shepherded them back into the minibus.

'Bye bye to you all.' Her gloved fingertips were offered to each of us in turn. 'Sandy did have a lovely Christmas. A big dinner with all the trimmings. The Queen's Speech. And then – for my treat – he joined in a reading of *Macbeth*.'

17

Old Soldiers

From my cottage I can look across the open fields of Tiny Palmer's farm to Severnham Hill. When I arrived, there was not a house in sight. Only a footpath climbed the hill towards woods which dated back to medieval times.

By some legal sleight of hand our all-powerful Councillor Conrad Twist had Severnham Hill declared an area of outstanding natural beauty, then proceeded to build ten houses on it. He himself took up residence in the first and best south-facing property, while the others were sold to locally important people.

As if this was not sufficient demonstration of his power, he had the path made into a well-surfaced lane and continued it down the far side of the hill to the council offices. When that was done he put up Private notices at both ends in order to deter casual traffic.

'After all,' Twist argued, 'it is an area of outstanding natural beauty.'

Thus the common herd might walk up the hill and on to the medieval woods, but motorists were discouraged to spoil the vista enjoyed by our chief councillor and his neighbours.

The story I am about to relate concerns his nearest neighbour – Lieutenant-General Wellesley Midwinter and, even more so, the formidable housekeeper Mrs Fenella Wardell. It was, as will be revealed, a most curious affair.

I first heard about General Midwinter and Mrs Wardell from Mr Spinks our village grocer. Like me Edward Spinks had escaped from London so we had much in common. Apart from being a good grocer, Edward and his wife Elizabeth became friends of mine. They often asked me to their flat above the High Street store and I shall tell more about them later.

Edward brought my groceries round on his usual morning and, as always, I enquired if he would care for a cup of coffee. It was an offer Edward seldom accepted, being a busy man, but on this occasion he nodded eagerly.

'Glad you offered. I need it.'

Over coffee, Edward said he had been to visit the new people at No. 2 Upper Severnham Lane and I asked,

'What happened to the Parker-Pearses?'

'Lloyd's Names,' Edward replied. 'Lost everything. Obliged to sell up and move out. Our dear chief councillor had to be careful who moved in next door to him. He seems to have solved that problem by having a retired General no less.'

'Really?'

'General Wellesley Midwinter. A Fighting General at one time. Headed NATO's Northern Command. He has yet to arrive. What happened was I called at No 2 after delivering some wine and cheese for Hilda's fortnightly meeting with her Severnham Ladies. I was seen by a Mrs Wardell the Housekeeper and I am still in a state of shock.'

'Sounds interesting,' I said because Edward Spinks was the mildest of people – a dapper, affable man. He went on,

'I left my car at the gate and walked to the front door. After ringing twice, a formidable looking woman – who must have been very attractive in her youth – answered. When I introduced myself, she told me tradespeople went to back doors and shut the front one. In my face.'

'Good Lord! Did you go to the back?'

'I was selling,' Edward laughed. 'I went and rang the back door bell and the same woman took her time to appear. She heard me out then told me what she called her terms and conditions. Instant responses. Immediate deliveries. Competitive prices. No mistakes. No apologies.'

'Did you accept?'

'I accepted her first order. A very large one. To be delivered this afternoon. At three-thirty. Precisely.'

'She's going to run you ragged, Edward.'

'Let's see. Perhaps we'll tame her.'

I doubted it. When Edward looked in a week later, he said with a rueful grin,

'Well, I've got through my first week with Mrs

Wardell. She did not treat me too badly – only had complaints on about half what I delivered. At the moment she is busy dealing with the painter and decorator, plumber and electrician, gardener and window cleaner.'

Tales about Mrs Wardell filtered down to me from various sources. How she made the painter completely re-paint the sitting room because the colours she had selected were not as she visualised. How she sent the plumber packing and had the electrician rewire half the house. Incidentally, Mrs Wardell passed the bill to Conrad Twist – but that is another story.

General Midwinter duly arrived and in fact I saw him before his housekeeper. Samuel Hopskip and I were working in our respective gardens when a tall straight figure came marching along the lane. There was no doubt we were seeing a general. The direct gaze, the clipped moustache, the firm chin all told of self discipline and high command.

'Good morning Sir,' I said as he strode past.

'Marning,' said Hopskip.

General Midwinter's acknowledgement was midway between a bark and a grunt. Then he did an extraordinary thing. On reaching the church lychgate, the old soldier about turned on the spot and came marching back towards us again. This time we stared while he strode past. After that we watched as he went up the lane to Severnham Hill. Although the upper lane is steep, the general never slowed down until he reached his gate and disappeared from our view.

'That was a smart about turn,' I remarked to Samuel.

'Oh ah,' my neighbour replied, cleaning his spade. 'I must go tell Evangeline. Her likes a good laugh.'

The general took to making this walk twice daily. We estimated the distance from his house to the lychgate was about a mile. Therefore there and back twice a day amounted to four miles. He never entered the church-yard let alone went further into the village. His brisk about turn sent him back past my cottage and up Severnham Hill.

General Midwinter arrived in midsummer and we expected him to cut down on his routine as October turned to November. But such was not the case. Layers of tweed and wax garments were added against autumn chills then frost, sleet and snow. He kept marching past, stamping round and striding back the way he had come. As the villagers agreed,

'You've got to hand it to him.'

By then I had met Mrs Wardell, though she neither noticed nor acknowledged my existence. I had called into Spinks Stores after lunch. Elizabeth was serving Mrs Prosser, the doctor's wife, and Edward came out of the back to attend to me. At that moment the door bell rang and Mrs Wardell stamped into the place. She said to Edward,

'There you are! I want every one of these items delivered before four this afternoon.'

A list was thrust past me into Edward's hand.

'Will you excuse me a moment . . ?' he started saying to her, but I knew my friend would not get away with it.

'Before four,' Mrs Wardell repeated.

Edward Spinks took his time studying the list then informed Mrs Wardell, 'All these are American drinks.'

'Because they are for Americans.'

'It'll mean my going into Gloucester.'

'That is immaterial to me,' said Mrs Wardell, 'so long as every item reaches the back door before four.'

Without further discussion, she turned and marched out of the store.

'Charming!' remarked Mrs Prosser.

'Are you going to do it, Edward?' Elizabeth asked.

'If you can hold the fort, my dear. I don't like to be beaten and . . . it's a big order.'

Edward Spinks left straight away for the warehouse in Gloucester and his heavily laden estate car returned past the cottage at about twenty to four. About an hour afterwards, three American staff cars drew up outside my front gate.

'Say feller,' the leading driver addressed me, 'you gotta Brit general living round here?'

'General Midwinter? No. 2 Upper Severnham Lane?'

'Dat's de guy. But it's all goddamn lanes. Which is what you said?'

'Up there,' I pointed. 'Second house along.'

We learned later how some of the general's NATO colleagues paid him a brief visit for old times and liquid refreshments.

There were other visitors – Germans, Danes, Canadians and more Americans. An army staff car called a couple of times. Our village postman kept us abreast with the general's letters and parcels – mainly from Whitehall, Aldershot plus places in and around Brussels.

Meanwhile the two brisk walks continued daily. They went on through the second summer and into the following autumn. One week there was incessant rain, but the general marched past and back again as if nothing untoward was happening.

I do not know how it was done but, despite his

remoteness and Mrs Wardell's arrogance, the villagers managed to find out a great deal about both of them. General Midwinter, we learned, was married and had three grown-up daughters. The separation had proved acrimonious and his wife's family, being high up in the Services, helped block his future career.

Another factor was Fenella Wardell. The wife of an army corporal, she and Midwinter had become lovers while he was a colonel at Aldershot. They had kept together before and after he retired despite all difficulties. While at Severnham, they went on two holidays together – for a fortnight in Denmark and a month to Canada.

Each small revelation was piled on the rest like building bricks until the villagers thought they saw the full structure. However there was more to come and the bricks began to be dismantled during the general's second winter at Severnham.

The first sign was a visit by Dr Prosser to No. 2 Upper Severnham Lane. This was followed by a second, third and fourth call. Mrs Wardell dealt with everything, summoning medical aid and having prescriptions delivered. November went by with the general remaining an invalid. That December was the same month when Sandy Porritt came to stay with me.

'How is the general?' Edward Spinks asked Mrs Wardell as he delivered a week's supply of groceries.

'The general,' she replied, 'is in the hands of his Doctor.' End of conversation.

Thus Christmas came and went – the Christmas of our pantomime, of Sandy's prodigious efforts and his sad departure during early January. General Midwinter, immured in his house on Severnham Hill, was temporarily forgotten.

Its location allowed me to see how an upstairs bedroom light came on at dusk and often during the night. I concluded the general was there fighting his last battle. In all fairness to the neighbours – Conrad and Hilda Twist at No 1, also the others – every offer of help was repudiated. Mrs Wardell made it quite clear their kind attentions were not required.

The villagers noted nevertheless how certain strangers were beginning to call. There were two swarthy gipsy-like men, driving a Jaguar, who stopped my neighbour and asked the way.

'Rough they were,' said Samuel, 'in smooth suits.'

Then there was the black man, built like a heavyweight boxer, who asked me the same. These out-of-character visitors began to put in brief but increasing appearances.

'What do you make of them?' I asked Edward Spinks.

'Something to do with her,' he said. 'Yet I've got to hand it to Mrs Wardell, she's doing all that can be done. She has Doctor Prosser, the district nurse, the chemist and everyone else concerned jumping when she says jump. Prosser wanted to move the general into hospital, but she refused.'

'Strange?'

'No. Doctor Prosser admits the general is as good at home as anywhere. Perhaps the old boy will get through his illness. After all he was a Fighting General.'

A couple of days later I was having coffee with Andy and Dottie Mead when Mrs Wardell called at the vicarage. Andy took her into his study leaving Dottie and me looking at each other.

'Why should she call here?' I wondered.

'Maybe she wants Andy to visit the general.'

'Has he ever been to any of the services?'

'No, but that wouldn't worry Andy.'

'Well, of course not.'

We went on drinking our coffees. Usually Mrs Wardell did not linger wherever she went. Her visit to the vicarage however took a long time. At last we heard her leaving and Andy Mead returned to us. He looked thoughtful.

'She wants him buried in the churchyard,' Andy said as Dottie poured fresh coffee. Dottie's hand shook.

'Alive?' she exclaimed.

'No, no!' Andy, usually the mildest of men, sounded irritable. His mind was still on the recent conversation. 'General Midwinter is in a coma. Has been for two days. Doctor Prosser told Mrs Wardell there is little chance of recovery.'

'Where there's life . . . ' Dottie began. She placed the coffee in front of Andy. 'I think you ought to check with Prosser, don't you?'

'I shall, though you know our doctor. Prosser would not lend his hand to anything dubious. He himself told me Mrs Wardell is a most competent woman.'

'Too competent.'

'That's unChristian,' Andy objected. 'Prosser and the district nurse have said Mrs Wardell is doing splendidly. She is up most nights tending to the sick man. But she also has to think ahead.'

'Why here?' asked Dottie. 'Hasn't he got a real home?'

'The Army was his home.'

'Then let the Army look after him.'

'He left specific orders with her to request burial in

26

Severnham churchyard. After a military funeral. It's in his will which she showed me. Like the funeral arrangements, the general has left everything to Mrs Wardell.'

I woke next morning before five because several cars in succession went past the cottage. Looking out I saw their lights crawl up the black bulk of Severnham Hill. More lights were on at the general's house. The cars reached the front, swung round and stopped. It could only mean one thing.

January and February are the months for country deaths, but those of Sandy Porritt and General Midwinter affected us more than normal.

'A general,' said Edward, 'is not your common or garden soldier.'

'We are all in His hands,' Andy reminded us. Our vicar seldom talked religion on weekdays so this remark was well noted.

'I wonder,' pondered Dottie, 'what Mrs Wardell will do?'

Nothing outwardly happened on the day of the general's death, though much must have gone on behind the scenes.

Hilda Twist told Elizabeth Spinks who told Edward who told me that Conrad and she had offered to help Mrs Wardell in any way they could. 'Despite the rebuffs we experienced,' Hilda added. Apparently the housekeeper thanked Hilda 'quite civilly' and said everything was in hand.

'What happens next?' I asked Edward.

'The funeral's on Thursday,' he told me. 'A military one.'

'They haven't put in an appearance as yet.'

'Oh they'll be here. He was in the real Army.'

I had to work at home next day and, before making a start, went round to the Hopskips for some eggs. Their back gate is nearer to the church than my front one. We were talking in the kitchen when there was a shout outside sounding like 'Sah!'

Samuel, Evangeline and I looked at each other. We resumed our important discussion, on the relative merits of eggs with brown shells as compared with those of white shells, when we heard two 'Sahs'. This drew us out of the kitchen and across the Hopskips back yard to the gate. Nearby was an army vehicle and two soldiers. Both vehicle and soldiers were camouflaged.

One of the soldiers had a crown on his shoulder while the other wore three stripes. The first carried a short leather covered stick, the second a clipboard, ballpoint pen and tape measure. The major kept pointing and talking in a strangulated sort of voice. The sergeant kept shouting out 'Sah!' They were making arrangements for the forthcoming funeral.

'We'll have the gun carriage turn here, Sergeant.'

'Sah!'

'And stop by the lychgate.'

'Sah!'

'The bearers will line up by that noticeboard.'

'Sah!'

'Funny caps they wear,' Evangeline whispered to me. 'With them shades down on their noses. Wonder they can see where they be marching to.'

Clearly the general's funeral was going to be a big occasion. In Severnham, such functions were headed by our Chief Councillor Conrad Twist. Thus we were not surprised when he put in an appearance. Twist was accompanied by his assistant Arthur Tremblett who, like the sergeant, carried a clipboard, ballpoint pen and tape measure.

'You're early,' Conrad said jovially.

'Never late,' the major brayed. 'We'll be wanting crowd control. Over one hundred and thirty in our party. Sergeant.'

'Sah!'

'How many in the band?'

'Sixteen Sah!'

'Call it one fifty.' Twist was informed.

'A good round number,' our councillor agreed. 'The villagers will have to keep well back. I have already notified my friend the Chief Constable. He should be along any moment.'

'Never early, eh?' the major brayed again and poked Twist in the ribs with the stick.

'The Laws delays.' Conrad Twist gave a superior chuckle causing the major to bray once more.

Presently the army and council representatives were joined by those of the police. Then the highways people arrived followed by electricians to put up a public address system. Gravediggers and florists started work. Clutching six eggs, I sidled past to the cottage and got on with mine.

Early on the morning of the funeral, Severnham Village was cut off from the outside world. The police and highways people put up diversion signs at the main road, also where the hill lane joins the one leading to the church. Those without passes wishing to reach the village had to make a detour via Lower Severnham and then they could only go as far as The Restoration Inn. At least pedestrians were able to get close to the church and I had a grandstand view from my cottage.

The army build-up during the hour before the service was impressive. Groups of personnel, who were obviously fully briefed, arrived and went about their various duties. There were military police in red caps, guards to line the route, bandsmen and riflemen.

At a quarter to eleven, the gun carriage with the coffin on it started down from the general's house. At the same time a long line of vehicles – staff cars and black limousines – came from the direction of the main road, but stopped where the hill lane joined that to the church. A great many people got out there, officers in magnificent uniforms and civilians in black. They formed up and waited for the gun carriage to reach them.

As those waiting began to follow the coffin, the band struck up a funeral march. Suddenly the solemnity of what we were seeing affected us all. Civilian men doffed their hats or caps. Women sniffed and dabbed their eyes with handkerchiefs. Even the most boisterous children looked pensive.

Walking immediately behind the gun carriage was an army chaplain and four tall women. They were the general's wife and three daughters. None wore hats and this, together with the black clothes, showed their faces to advantage. There was, to use an inept phrase, class there. Mrs Midwinter, a woman in her late sixties, had retained her thoroughbred looks. As for the daughters they were as beautiful as she still was.

Following them came a host of senior officers from a dozen or more nations. The villagers craned their necks to catch more of a sight which would only happen once in their lifetime. Our vicar was waiting for the chaplain at the lychgate. Together they led the coffin into the church. The Midwinter family and the rest of the ticket-only mourners came after them. These naturally included Councillor Conrad and Hilda Twist, solemn faced as befitted the occasion. Conrad had of course laid on the local press to record his part in the proceedings.

The service was relayed to those outside, including an address by the chaplain outlining General Midwinter's military career. As I could not catch this from the cottage, I slipped out and made my way round to where six riflemen and a lone trumpeter waited for the final salute. The crowd had left a space here and I was interested in two people standing by the open grave though well apart. One was Mrs Wardell, the other a tall raw-boned man who looked as if he had been a soldier. Neither the housekeeper nor the stranger glanced at each other.

Afterwards – after the heart-wringing Last Post and shots over the grave – three further events took place before the episode was finally closed. They explained and revealed a lot.

The reception was at the general's house. Councillor Twist made the arrangements with money from the Council's Hospitality Fund. Twist deemed it a justifiable village occasion – despite the absence of most other villagers. However Hilda and the Severnham Ladies were there in force to comfort the widow and the rest of the Midwinter family. Edward Spinks, who did the catering, spoke to me later and filled in the details.

'Very crowded. Very noisy. All those military types talking at the top of their voices.'

'What about Conrad and Hilda?'

'In their element.'

'And the Midwinters?'

31

'They stood apart. Went early.'

Which left me with the $64,000 question. How had Mrs Wardell dealt with the situation? After all, the house was now hers.

Edward could not help here. He said,

'She slid off following the funeral. Two gipsy-like men and a big black in a Jaguar came to collect her.'

Eventually the guests left and the army cleared up. By late afternoon it was as if nothing had happened – apart from the masses of flowers in Severnham churchyard.

The house remained dark and empty that night. Next morning a new Mrs Wardell arrived at Spinks Stores. Edward, Elizabeth and I stared as she walked in with a springy step. Normally Mrs Wardell wore sober clothes and long skirts. This time her top half was in a loose red pullover while below were shapely black stockinged legs. Her whole attitude had changed.

'Hello Mr Spinks!' Fenella Wardell called to him. 'I have another long list for you to pull the stops out. My party's tonight.'

Edward glanced at us then took the list and studied it. As he was doing so, Fenella Wardell appeared to see Elizabeth and me for the first time. Wonder of wonders she smiled and wiggled her red nailed fingers in our direction.

'Yes, I can do this,' Edward said. 'When do you want it?'

'Sooner the better, Mr Spinks. Must rush. Lots to do.'

We watched her go. Round-eyed. Open-mouthed.

The cars started rolling up early afternoon. By evening the party at No. 2 Upper Severnham Lane was in full swing. The music grew louder and louder. One did not have to be a betting man to know Councillor Twist would object.

He did and so did the other prestigious people. Failing to get the sound turned down, Police Constable Stan Oakshott was summoned. Later we learned how he had been met by the big black man who said,

'We're having a party, man. Either join us or leave us.'

After that the Chief Constable was contacted and he sent along two of his Gloucestershire Constabulary. So the story goes, they were greeted by enthusiastic half-naked girls wanting rides in their car. Later, at the police canteen, the two constables said it had been the toughest assignment of their career – escaping *virgo intacta*. And the party went on.

By nightfall, a pop group arrived with loudspeakers like aircraft hangars. The whole of Severnham was treated to the music. What it must have sounded to Conrad and Hilda Twist, living a hundred yards away, does not bear contemplation. No wonder they left to spend the night with their estate agent son Jason Twist and, no doubt, they made fearful plans.

Stories of Fenella Wardell's party abound. How Tiny Palmer went to remonstrate with them and was brought back dead drunk at dawn. How the partygoers formed a chain and ran whooping round the other Upper Severnham houses and gardens. How the black man carried two local ladies into the medieval woods. How the fire in the Twists shed was started and how the firemen joined the party.

Came the dawn and silence. During the morning, the partygoers slipped away in their cars. They included Fenella who, as a matter of interest, sold the house back to the Twists at a reasonable sum. Severnham never saw her again, though she left us intrigued. There is only one piece to add and that fell into place a week later.

I was walking past the churchyard when I saw the tall raw-boned man by the general's grave. He had tidied up the site and we fell into conversation. What the man told me was intriguing.

Apparently they all stemmed from Aldershot – he, Fenella, the gipsy-like pair, the black and General Wellesley Midwinter. He came from an army family. She was a sergeant's daughter. The swarthy men warrant officers. The black a boxing champion. I asked the tall man his name. It was Jim Wardell. Fenella's husband.

'We all grew up in and around the regiment,' Jim Wardell related over a cup of coffee. 'Fenella was the most attractive girl there. When she became a woman every man lusted after her, I can tell you. I was supposed to be the lucky one.' He paused.

'And?' I prompted.

'Was at first,' he continued, 'but I knew our madcap colonel had his eyes on her. Like the rest. And she knew. They always know. Then the regiment went to the Middle East. To sort out a little problem. There the colonel laid his life on the line to save mine. No sooner had we got back when he took her away from me. Just like that.'

'Didn't do him no good,' Wardell continued. 'From the Army's point of view I mean. Yes, he became a general through putting his life on the line again and again. He always led from the front. The whole of Aldershot knew it. As did the MOD. They used him, but he was never accepted. I'll say this for Fenella and him. Stuck together. Until the end.'

'Where now?' I asked as Jim Wardell finished his coffee and rose to leave.

'Aldershot,' he said. We walked to his car. He looked thoughtful while opening the door. 'I'd have her back,' Jim told me, 'but she wouldn't consider it. Got a will on her has Fenella. A will of iron. As the general had. I have to admit they were meant for each other.' His voice was husky. All of a sudden he got into the car, started the engine and drove away.

When I relayed this conversation to Edward Spinks he said,

'People don't realise soldiers are different. They are willing to die for the rest of us. To put their lives on the line as Wardell said. At any time. One must make allowances for them.'

Mean Men

People often ask me, 'from where do I get my stories'? The glib yet true answer is by looking and listening. I can even gaze out of my study window and see them unfolding.

Tiny Palmer has just driven past in a new pick-up truck. His 250 acre farm lies across the lane from the front of my cottage. It is partly arable, but the cream of the cream comes from his prize herd of Jersey cows. Most farmers plead poverty. Tiny however, who is very comfortably off, has made it into an art form. He enjoys the reputation of being the meanest man in the Severn Valley.

First, what does he looks like? Tiny is in fact well over

six feet tall, broad-shouldered, athletic and has an innocent peasant face denoting extreme cunning. Summer and winter he wears red check shirts tucked into blue jeans tucked into green rubber boots. Admittedly his winter shirts are padded, but the overall image remains the same.

On the surface, Tiny is rosy-cheeked, forever smiling and slapping people on the back. He is a very physical person. This can include knocking someone down from time to time as, apart from being strong, he has a quick temper. For example, Tiny will accept free drinks for ever, but it would be a brave man who suggests Palmer buys the next round. Only strangers do this and only foolish strangers make the same mistake twice.

That said, Tiny's half-timbered home is a picture of what a farmhouse should look like. This is due to Janis, his always cheerful wife. Janis sees to the hens, the pigs and a small farm shop from which she makes pin money. As for the children, there is a bit of a mystery with the first – Laurie, a loutish version of Tiny. Gossip says Laurie was by a Gloucester market woman. Later Janis produced two lovely children in holy wedlock – a boy and a girl resembling Botticelli angels.

But back to Tiny's mean ways. I witnessed an example well before beginning to hear the stories. During my first summer in Severnham, I went to the church fête. There was an ice cream stall and a big man (Tiny Palmer) approached it ahead of me. He was accompanied by two children, a boy and a girl.

'Large cornet,' said Tiny, who then found he did not have sufficient change. 'Pay you later,' he told the ice cream lady after licking the cornet. As he turned away, I noticed the mouths of the boy and girl go down.

'What about us, Dad?' asked the boy. By way of a reply, Tiny enquired,

'Where's your pocket money?'

At the time I was pleased to see a cheerful woman (Janis) come up to the children and buy them a cornet apiece.

Janis had a good laugh at what the kids told her. She placated them by promising,

'Wait till I get him home.'

Shortly after the summer fête, I met Tiny Palmer in The Restoration. He had seen me at the cottage and I had seen him on the farm so we introduced ourselves. I then bought him a pint of best bitter and another after he downed the first.

'Thirsty work farming,' was all I said for him to push his empty glass towards Polly the barmaid.

I finished my drink while Tiny continued talking to Polly. When we both had empty glasses, I waited. Eventually Tiny remarked he was on his way to Gloucester Market and left.

'Thanks for the drink,' he said in the singular.

'Did you expect Tiny to buy you one in return?' Polly asked.

'Well, not any more.'

'Or ever. He is so mean! Do you know, Tiny never pays a bill until he gets the final notice? The electricity, water and telephone people are always threatening to cut him off. As for paying his rates, he is the despair of the council office.'

About a week later, Edward Spinks brought me my groceries and mentioned he had some for Palmer's Farm.

'Do you deliver there?' I asked, which in Severnham-speak means, 'How do you get paid?'

'Fortunately,' said Edward, 'I deal with Janis.'

Edward Spinks accepted coffee and told me more about Tiny's many meannesses. Like me, our grocer was ex-London. Now, living in the country, we indulged in village gossip.

About a month later I visited Severn Valley Farmers to make some purchases. I kept on looking because Tiny and Janis Palmer were there to buy an Aga cooker. Barney the mischievous and crafty storekeeper attended to them.

'You've got yourself a sale,' I heard Tiny say to Barney. 'When can we have it?'

'There is,' Barney replied, 'the matter of payment.'

'Don't be silly,' said Tiny. 'You know me.'

'Oh ah,' came the comment which, when translated in this case means, 'Only too well.'

'You can put it on my account, Barney.'

'It's over the limit.'

'Then send me a bill.'

'Against SVF policy.'

'Who says so?'

'The owners.'

'But you're family. A director.'

'A humble one, Tiny. I'm afraid I can't. Look, if you want to think about it, I'll serve this gentleman first.'

'He's no gentleman!' Tiny Palmer had to laugh at his own joke. 'Lives near to me.'

How Janis got her Aga I do not know, but she did. I saw it in her farmhouse kitchen some time later – beside the washing machine, tumble drier, dishwasher, refrigerator, deep freezer and the rest.

Next came the story of the gentlemen farmers' barn. The first gentleman farmer was a rich townie who bought a nearby farm. His name was Jardine. He informed The Restoration one Sunday morning how the place had been purchased 'as an investment', also 'to please the little woman'. Mrs Jardine was a monstrous creature with a penchant for fur coats which made her larger still. She spent two weekends at the farm before announcing her preference for Golders Green.

The first gentleman farmer then found a second gentleman farmer – a retired colonel called Haggard – whose wife wanted riding stables. What she did not want was 'that dirty old barn'. The two gentlemen farmers consulted The Restoration about the barn and Tiny Palmer offered to help them.

'I'll see you're all right,' he beamed as they lined up drinks for him, 'if you'll co-operate to our mutual advantage.'

Tiny told them he was looking for such a barn, but the dismantling, transporting and reassembling costs were too much for him to bear. Before they could buy him two more pints, the pair of gentlemen farmers had agreed to split the costs.

'Can't say fairer than that,' they took it in turns to assure him. The rest of us looked on in amazement mixed with admiration.

'Do you know,' Edward Spinks told me later, 'after he had put up and painted the barn, Tiny sent each of them the bill for the paint and labour. Would you believe it, both paid.'

In order to continue with the Tiny Palmer saga, it is necessary to move backwards in time and introduce a few more Flukes.

At the lower end of the village there is a rundown garage and workshop which once belonged to one Tobias Fluke. These establishments began as sheds which Tobias took over from his father Zacharias shortly after World War II. Tobias Fluke had an army career mending tank tracks so he decided to apply his acquired skills to motor cars and farm machinery.

Mind you, as the villagers would say, Tobias started off with a few disadvantages. To begin with he did not like work, preferring to smoke pipes and pass his days with whoever wanted a good chinwag. A perfect day to him consisted of two morning pipes and two afternoon pipes with a long midday session at The Piggy, when he generally smoked an in-between pipe.

As for actual garage work, well most villagers were rather reluctant to let Tobias near their cars. He tended to bash out dents and straighten bumpers, as he had once done on tanks, while his spray painting looked like camouflage. These details did not endear him to discerning owners. Eventually, the garage was reduced to serving petrol and stocking spare parts.

Tobias had three sons – Alec, Brian and Chris. As Maud the mother had to go out and do cleaning work – to try and raise family finances above poverty level – the three boys were brought up in the garage and adjoining workshop.

The garage and workshop situation remained unchanged when the lads reached their teens, then early twenties. Tobias continued to enjoy his pipes and chinwags. Maud still slaved away at wherever there was lowly paid work. Gradually their resentment built up against the old man.

'When we inherit the family business,' Alec and Brian

would say, 'everything is going to change.' They had done poorly at school unlike quiet Chris. Thus the two elder sons proceeded from unlearned lessons to non-careers, while Chris went to technical college and specialised in computers.

To cut a sub-story short, the time came for Tobias Fluke to leave this world. He did so with a bang – trying to weld up a petrol tank. It was a relief to the family, also to the rest of the Flukes who liked to make the most of a funeral. As Maud sat between Alec and Brian, alternately mourning and drinking, they reassured her,

'Don't worry Mum.'

'Your troubles are over.'

'We'll run the business.'

'And start making real money.'

They began well by cleaning the sheds, painting new signs and printing business cards with the title 'Director' after their names. There was only one small snag. No new business materialised. What with the funeral expenses and entertaining, the cash flow situation was worse than ever.

Alec and Brian's next step was a tempting but false one. Various sales representatives used to call at the garage and workshop making all kinds of irresistible offers. A picture was painted of the Fluke firm becoming local stockists for farm and garden machinery. Shiny new items of equipment, from chain saws to ride-on mowers, began appearing along the garage forecourt.

'There's no need to dirty our hands with old cars and bits of machinery,' the brothers told each other, also their mother. 'We'll display brand new products for sale at high profits and start making some real money.'

The trouble was they did not sell a single item

because stores in nearby towns offered the same goods at low margins. After a few weeks the shiny new equipment began to look old as well as dusty. Their cash flow situation was worse than ever.

A village story went round at the time which I found hard to believe, but everyone swore was true. According to the tale, the last words Tobias Fluke had said to Alec and Brian were,

'Never do business with Tiny Palmer.'

It sounds apocryphal to me, however what happened next went like this.

We were suffering high winds rushing up the Severn Vale as if it was a wind tunnel. Apart from bringing down twigs and branches, the winds could and did uproot whole trees. Two old ashes were dislodged at Palmer's Farm and one actually lay across his front drive.

Brian Fluke was the first at the garage next morning. He was trying to deal with a blown down sign and a badly sprung door when the telephone started to ring. It kept ringing as Brian desperately fought his way into the garage.

'Hello Brian,' came the cheerful version of Tiny Palmer's voice. 'I bet you're selling a lot of chain saws?'

'Oh ah,' Brian said although, to date, they had not sold a single one. He wondered what Tiny was on about.

'Because of these winds,' Tiny explained. 'Bringing down trees.'

'Oh ah.'

'I might be in the market myself,' Palmer went on. 'For a big saw to cut up tree trunks and a little one to deal with the branches.'

'Oh ah.'

'Have you got any left, Brian?'

'One or two I think.'

'Any chance of you bringing out a couple and showing me? You're the chain saw expert round here.'

'Sure Tony. When would you like to see me?'

'Soon as possible. I've got to get to Gloucester, but the tree's blocking my drive.'

'I'll be right along. Give me ten minutes.'

'Give you five,' said Tiny Palmer who had the reputation of not giving away anything at all.

Brian Fluke put a large and small chain saw in the boot of his car then added a can of petrol and one of oil. He also took with him a demonstration kit which included a pair of overalls in the maker's colours. Halfway along the drive to Tiny's farmhouse, Brian came upon the fallen ash tree. He had put on the overalls and was filling up the chain saw tank when Tiny came out to him.

'See what I mean?' said Tiny.

'Oh ah.' Brian nodded. 'Soon clear this for you. These saws go through the hardest of woods like butter.'

A quarter of an hour later, the tree trunk had been cut into sections and rolled to one side of the drive.

'Great job!' said Tiny. 'Now show me how the little saw works. Ash logs burn well in my living room fireplace.'

'Watch this,' Brian decided he would impress his first potential customer.

Within a further quarter of an hour he had cut the branches and most of the trunk into fire logs.

'Terrific!' Tiny seemed delighted. It was the ideal time, as Brian later told Alec, 'to close the sale'. But Tiny Palmer had another suggestion. The other tree in fact.

'It's been loosened,' he indicated a second ash further towards his house. 'I don't think it'll fall across the drive,

but it's got to come down. Let's see you fell a tree and –
you can cut that one up for firewood as well.'

It was the remark 'you can cut that one up for
firewood as well' which alerted Brian. He looked Tiny in
the eye and asked,

'Are you going to buy these two chains saws?'

'Let's see the second tree come down and cut up.'

'I think you're having me on.'

'I want to go to Gloucester Market, Brian.'

'No one's stopping you, Tiny.'

'You are,' Palmer countered, 'by not getting on with
it.'

They had reached an impasse. Brian Fluke was certain
he had been deceived. Tiny Palmer wanted to milk the
situation for all it was worth. When Brian refused to do
any more, unless the two chain saws were purchased,
Tiny tried a different line of approach. He remarked,

'You don't expect me to buy a couple of old demonstration models, do you?'

'They're not old demonstration models!' Brian shouted at him. 'They are factory new.'

'I find that hard to believe,' said Tiny glancing at the
saws now covered in oily sawdust. 'Who are you trying
to kid, Brian? I wouldn't give you a fiver for both of
them.'

'I don't want a fiver, Tiny. I want full prices.'

'You're joking.'

'I'm not.'

'Then I'll get myself off to Gloucester Market.' With
that Tiny Palmer turned and left a furious Brian Fluke.

When Brian returned to the garage he saw Alec and
told him of the situation. Alec was angrier still and
insisted they go back at once to confront Tiny Palmer.

However, by the time they reached the farmhouse, no one was there. Tiny had long left for Gloucester Market and Janis taken the children off to school. Janis would then do a little shopping and afterwards a lot of gossiping in the best Severnham tradition.

'Is that the second tree?' Alec asked Brian.

'Oh ah.'

'I reckon if you looped a rope over one of them upper branches and pulled . . . '

'And you cut a deep vee in the base . . . ' Brian nodded.

'It would come down right across Tiny's effing drive.'

This is what they did. The second ash tree was larger than the first. It completely blocked the drive at an awkward spot which Tiny could not avoid. Laughing like a couple of schoolkids, Alec and Brian packed away the saws and returned to their garage.

As the day went by, their triumphant mood was replaced by one of foreboding. Tiny Palmer was not a man to cross. He was also a big and physical person who could and did deliver hard knocks. During their liquid lunch at The Piggy, Alec and Brian told Garnet Fluke of the situation. They hoped he would rally the rest of the Flukes behind them, but all he said was,

'You're fools.'

It was late afternoon when Tiny Palmer's pick-up truck skidded to a stop on the forecourt of the Flukes garage. Tiny leapt out and came straight into the office where Alec and Brian stood shoulder to shoulder awaiting him.

'Which one of you,' he shouted, 'dropped my tree across my drive?'

'Brian told me you wanted it down,' answered Alec.

'So we cut it down,' Brian added.

'You did, did you?' Tiny swung a punch at Brian who tried to duck. This caused the punch to graze him and hit Alec. Then the two Flukes started swinging punches at Tiny. He managed to grasp Brian round the middle and the three men fell wrestling to the floor. A furious fight ensued with Tiny butting Brian and Alec raining blows on to Palmer's head.

Eventually all three were out of breath and drew apart.

'You are going to cut up that tree,' said Tiny.

'No way,' Alec retorted.

'If you will agree to buy the saws . . . ' Brian began.

'No way!' Tiny shouted. He scrambled to his feet and so did the Fluke brothers. 'I'll have the tree moved and cut up without your old saws. You'll see. And you'd both better watch out. No one crosses me and gets away with it.'

'You can make a start,' said Alec, 'by getting off our premises.'

'Premises?' Tiny scoffed. 'You two are bloody jokes.'

What happened next could have been unhappy coincidences. At least I thought so. On the other hand, villagers looked expectant while discussing the feud.

About a week after the dust-up in the garage, an 'on sale or return' rotavator, left all night outside the Flukes' garage, was found covered in black paint. Alec promptly called in PC Stan Oakshott and made an accusation. Our worthy constable just as promptly mounted his bike and cycled up to Palmer's Farm. There Tiny denied any knowledge of the offence.

'Couldn't be bothered with them,' he said.

As it happened Stan, Tiny, Alec and Brian had all

attended the village school. They had grown up together. Knew each other only too well.

'Can I see your paint store?' Oakshott of The Yard asked. His police house was in a yard behind the council offices.

'Course you can,' said Tiny. 'Matter of fact I'm doing some painting at the moment.'

He was touching up iron brackets. With black paint.

'A coincidence.' Stan sucked his teeth. 'Look Tiny. Enough's enough.'

'I don't know what you mean.'

'You're even. Forget it. Let it rest.'

'What about the flipping Flukes?'

'I'll have a word with them,' Stan Oakshott promised. 'Make sure you all cool it.'

The feuding seemed to stop. Weeks went by with the Fluke brothers desperately seeking to succeed while Tiny Palmer kept on succeeding. In The Restoration and at Gloucester Market Tiny laughed about the Common Market and all its rules. In reality he looked on the EC as a money-making machine for farmers.

'Do you know,' Tiny said to Janis, 'we can get subsidies of £28 per ewe whether or not the ewes produce lambs?'

'Great!' said Janis more absorbed in her *Hello* magazine.

'I could easily put a hundred ewes in the top field. Being on Severnham Hill, that would make me a hill farmer. It would also earn us a cool £2,800.'

'Super!' Janis agreed.

This is what Tiny did. The village applauded his acumen and other farmers began to read EC rules with more interest.

That is until one night someone left the gate to the top field open. By morning the hundred ewes had trampled and eaten their way round the gardens of Conrad Twist and his neighbours. It took Tiny all day to return the ewes to the field. He firmly believed Alec and Brian Fluke were to blame. However, as PC Stan Oakshott pointed out, there was no proof. Moreover, the Flukes claimed to have been at a skittles match.

There was an interesting sequel to this incident. The top people, comprising councillors, solicitors and accountants who lived on Severnham Hill, sent Tiny Palmer a bill for damages. It came to over £900. He argued about it for months.

During these turbulent times affecting the Fluke brothers and their mother, the third brother Chris quietly went on with his computer studies. He showed an aptitude for electronics and their applications. After doing well at technical college Chris worked for a computer services company in Cheltenham.

As soon as he started working, Chris paid his mother so she no longer had to accept lowly jobs. He also sought out a friendly bank manager and together they devised the strategy for his future business. Alec and Brian listened tolerantly because their big break was always just round the next corner. Young Chris, they told themselves and their mother, is still wet behind the ears.

Young Chris merely grinned. He knew the world was changing and he meant to move with it. Could he, Chris asked Alec and Brian, have the unused workshop next to their garage for his computer work? Laughing, they let him use the place. Rent free.

'Provided you clean it up a bit,' said Alec.

This Chris did and more. He cleared everything out of

the shed, scraped and painted, fitted white work tops and shelves, then – helped by his friendly bank manager – purchased tools and test equipment.

'Very impressive,' said Brian, 'but where's your business coming from?'

'I've already got service contracts,' Chris replied, 'from the local bank and the doctor's surgery.'

That was only the beginning. The computer age had even come to Severnham. Suddenly everyone who was anyone thereabouts seemed to be acquiring personal computers and word processors. The branch library had one. The police sub-station had another. Misses Menage and Nook bought a simple system for the school. Andy Mead did the same at the vicarage. Then wonder of wonders Conrad Twist agreed to let a Fluke – in the efficient person of Chris – look after Severnham District Council's computers.

By then the Fluke garage had been cleared of all motor car and agricultural accessories. It became a computer showroom with a communications and photocopying annexe. Alec and Brian did deliveries. Their mother, transformed by hair care and new clothes, looked after the office. Everyone was impressed and said so – with the grudging exception of Tiny Palmer. Yet one day, he too appeared in the showroom.

'Can I help you?' asked Chris.

'Just looking,' Tiny replied. 'This model you have here for £1899 could handle all my farm accounts.'

'It could indeed,' Chris confirmed. 'It has a 66 Mhz processor, 250 Mb hard drive and 4Mb Ram.'

'Yeah,' said Tiny, 'but the price you're asking is way over the top. I've been to the big boys in Cheltenham and Gloucester. They've quoted me £1699. Can you beat them?'

'I'm afraid not,' Chris smiled, 'but, when you buy, make sure you get the equivalent model.'

Tiny bought what he thought was the equivalent model for £200 less and, at first, all went well. An intelligent man, he studied the handbook and tutorial disk before feeding his farm accounts and records into the computer. Once that was done, it became in his words 'dead simple'. Tiny told his cronies at The Restoration and Gloucester Market that he could not see how the so-called computer experts could justify their existences.

Then one evening – four days after the guarantee ran out – Tiny was feeding some items into his computer when everything became tangled. The more he tried to clear the data, the worse it became. Although the hour was late, he rang Chris Fluke and told him what had happened.

'Could you come out and fix it?' Tiny enquired.

'Certainly,' Chris replied, 'but it'll cost you £50 mind.'

'What? What for?'

'There's a call-out charge of £25 and the test charge is the same.'

'Oh,' Tiny said after a pause. 'It's late. What if I bring the system in to you first thing tomorrow morning?'

'There'll be just the test charge.'

'Mm. I'll think about it,' said Tiny.

Tiny Palmer fretted all night and at nine next morning rang the supplier in Gloucester. There a bored young woman said goods requiring servicing, particularly those out of guarantee, had to go to the manufacturer's workshop in Bristol.

'How much will it cost?'

'Two hundred pounds approximately.'

'What? What for?'

'A hundred pounds to cover transportation and insurance. A hundred pounds for dismantling, inspection, rectification and testing. That's the minimum and of course there's VAT.'

At this point Tiny slammed down the phone. Ten minutes later he arrived at Chris's shop with the defective computer.

'It sounds like your PD3K,' said Chris placing the unit on a bench and taking off a panel.

'My what?' asked Tiny who was watching very carefully.

'This,' said Chris sliding out a circuit board and unplugging a tiny component.

'Have you got a replacement?'

'No.' Chris shook his head. 'Your Mk I model was obsolete when you bought it. We stocked the Mk II, now the Mk III. I could however get you a PD3K from Cheltronic Spares if you like. Only cost you a couple of quid.'

'I could do that myself,' said Tiny picking up the pieces and walking out of the workshop. Chris watched him go without rancour. He even waved Tiny a friendly goodbye.

Tiny drove straight to the spares supplier, bought a PD3K for £1.65 and drove triumphantly home with it. He plugged the component into the board and slid the latter into its frame.

'Up the Flukes!' Tiny told Janis as he switched on.

This time the letters and figures were not only

jumbled, they ran from line to line changing as they went.

Chris was in his workshop when Tiny drew up outside. The Flukes watched the erring computer being unloaded again and glanced uneasily at each other. Only Chris looked unperturbed.

'Still in trouble?' he greeted Tiny.

'You told me a PD3K . . . ' Palmer began.

'Since then,' Chris nodded with sympathy, 'I have been asking round the trade. Your cheap computer was a rogue model. The makers tried a PD3K, then a PL4C as plug-ins, before they settled for a soldered SMR55 on the Mk II. You were lucky your Mk I lasted over a year.'

'All right Chris,' Palmer said. 'You win. Can my computer be put right and what will it cost?'

'The answer to your first question is yes by four o'clock this afternoon. I would also give you a six months trouble free warranty.' Chris picked up a calculator and tapped the buttons. 'The answer to your second question is £178.36p including VAT.'

'One hundred and seventy-eight pounds?' Tiny was appalled.

'And thirty-six pence,' Chris nodded. 'I'll have the bill made out, but I shall want it in cash.'

Success Story

I am fond of Severnham folk, but the ones with whom I have most rapport are the Spinks. This is partly because we all came from London and have an extra viewpoint. In addition, the Spinks are pleasant, helpful and generous. They do a great deal for the community in their quiet way. Many a poor person has been helped by them – with the minimum of fuss.

Let me begin by describing their setting because that is of interest in itself. During the Middle Ages, Severnham was centred round the church end of the village. Where the Spinks now have their shop stood an outlying farm. Later, in Georgian times, the farm was acquired and converted by a rich corn merchant as the family house. Then, at the turn of this century, it was bought and changed again into a general store.

Traces of those conversions can be seen by entering Spinks Store through the central front entrance. What used to be a hall, with ground floor rooms on either side, was all knocked into one. At the same time, the tall windows looking out at the High Street were replaced with much wider bay ones. Inside there is plenty of light and space.

The long counter, behind which the Spinks serve, is on the left, while to the right there are display shelves and a large old cast iron stove kept lit throughout the winter. The place has central heating, but the stove is a popular feature.

To the right also, there is a door opening into the family part of the house. This contains what is a new hall chiefly taken up by a straight staircase to the upstairs rooms. At the rear, partly under the stairs but overlooking the back yard and garden, is Edward Spinks' office. A glass panelled door leads outside.

Behind the house stands an original barn used by the shop as a store room. It is really old with timbers holding up as well as when they were put together. The barn store has a stone flagged floor supporting hefty wooden racks. Edward says he likes to work in there because he seems to feel those others who did so in the past.

Stretching from behind the barn lies a rectangle of sheds and stables. Some have been converted into extra storerooms, two are garages and the end stable remains as such. Within the rectangle, like the quad at a university college, there is stone paving then a lovely lawn. Flower beds have been added here and there to give a garden effect.

As for upstairs, the main room is over the shop. After that, the rest of the living quarters take the form of an extensive and rambling flat with further bedrooms in the attic. Elizabeth has over the years made the Spinks home comfortable and picturesque. Her eye for good furniture and materials, for the right decorations and pictures in the right places, is evident wherever one goes.

Edward Spinks, as I have told before, is notable for his cherubic features and half glasses. He could play the part of Pickwick because he comes from that mould. Even when something solemn is taking place, Edward's sense of humour and goodwill keep bubbling up, ready to be released.

Elizabeth is taller than her husband and presents a first impression of being austere. This however is because Elizabeth is a caring and thoughtful person. She is the one who generally detects hardships and the need to act. For example, Elizabeth was very kind to Mrs Fluke – mother of Alec, Brian and Chris during their hard times.

The Spinks have two children, David and Jane. David looks like his mother. He is tall and serious, quiet and helpful. As for Jane, who does not resemble either of her parents, she is a blonde, whereas the other three are dark haired. She has eyes of light blue, while theirs are brown. Edward often jokes about it by saying,

'There was this fair-haired milkman when we were living in Kent.'

The Spinks seem to think I starve in my cottage and ask me to dinner at least once a month. I invite them back, but they prefer to entertain than be entertained. As Elizabeth puts it, 'One extra makes no difference'.

She likes cooking and, being the wife of a grocer, has every ingredient to hand.

A typical dinner at the Spinks is as follows. I would go round the back and meet David or Jane in the garden. David is fond of animals, every type of animal, and he usually has his latest acquisition to show me. These range from dogs and cats to some quite exotic creatures. As for Jane she is a horse lover and keeps her pony in the stable. She is usually there either cleaning tack, mucking out or bedding down – if not out riding around the district.

Edward is often in his office, doing a bit of book work prior to my arrival. We then proceed upstairs where Elizabeth welcomes us with sherries before returning to her cooking. While Edward and I chat, we hear David and Jane come in to lend a hand.

The meal when it arrives is wonderful. Elizabeth tries not to repeat herself and I do not think she has ever done so. Normally David and or Jane eat with us, but there is never any fuss about it. Afterwards comes the best part when Edward, Elizabeth and I sit back relaxing over coffees and liqueurs.

It is then they tell me many of the tales in this book or fill in the gaps. I was keen to hear their story, but they did not at first refer to life before Severnham. At long last my patience was rewarded and it came about in a strange way. Edward mentioned a visit to the dentist and Elizabeth said,

'No more grinding of teeth, thank goodness.'

'Elizabeth and I,' Edward told me, 'grew up in Sevenoaks. Her father was a schoolteacher, mine a bank manager. We did quite well at our respective schools. After that she went in for domestic science while I studied accountancy and commercial law. Our social lives revolved round tennis and cricket clubs.'

'Typical suburbans,' Elizabeth added and I said,

'Yes, I know.'

'I had my sights on a career in the City,' Edward went on, 'so I was delighted, after passing my final exams, to be accepted by Hayden Lowndes. Know them?' he asked me.

'Civil engineering,' I nodded. 'Fine company.'

'Old man Hayden,' Edward confirmed, 'was one of the best. A real City gentleman. His word was literally his bond. As for Lowndes, a truly original thinker. It was a pleasure working for them. Elizabeth and I got married on the strength of that appointment.'

'Edward kept on about it,' said Elizabeth, 'while he was supposed to be proposing to me.'

'Then what?' I prompted. 'Hayden Lowndes went public, didn't they?'

'Yes, and at first all was well. We used to concentrate on UK projects. Roads, bridges and tunnels. Infrastructure. The director who came in to look after the City's interests – he's dead and gone now – pushed us into overseas work. Mostly in the Middle East. It was lucrative, but dicey.

'By that time,' Edward continued, 'we had the children and I became Company Secretary. Another City figure joined our Board because we were going through a difficult patch in the Middle East. It was the period when business life began to change for the worse. The City of London has always been a mercenary place, but it had standards. Those were pushed aside and sheer greed became a virtue. Short termism a way of life. The cannibalization of British industry commenced.'

Edward Spinks paused and reflected. He was lost in thought until Elizabeth prompted him.

'The takeover,' she murmured.

'I seem to recall it,' I said.

'It's a wonder you do,' retorted Edward. 'There were so many. We were acquired by a much smaller outfit – UTI, Utility Trading Industries – aided and abetted by the financial press. Tim Bulston, now Sir Tim, was and still is the darling of the City. He proceeded to convert us into a conglomerate. Property development. Transport, offshore investments. You name it. Old man Hayden was pushed out. Lowndes left. Then Bulston brought in his fellow buccaneers. A smart arse accountant. A sharp lawyer. An awful ex-minister. A top PR man. After that it was takeovers and asset stripping all the way. There were also boxes at Ascot, Wimbledon and what have you. Why they kept me, I never knew at first. I thought Tim Bulston saw me as his acceptable face of capitalism.'

While Edward was speaking he stood up, went to a desk and brought me an unframed photograph. It showed him and Elizabeth in evening clothes with a man and a girl also formally dressed. The man I recognised as Sir Tim Bulston – a big smiling bully whose name was legendary in the City. The girl looked like his daughter.

'This was taken at the Savoy,' said Edward, 'celebrating Tim's knighthood. During the same week he was responsible for making 2000 people redundant in the north-east and selling the company's know-how to the Germans.'

I studied Bulston's grin which was belied by the piggy eyes, low forehead and grossly thick neck.

'The girl,' Elizabeth said, 'is Zelda. His second wife.'

'What happened to the first?' I asked.

'Oh, paid off.'

'The whole crowd of them,' said Edward, 'were on their second wives by then. Apart from mistresses, that is. It wasn't us.'

I knew what he meant.

'Yet Tim Bulston kept me on with all the perks. Health care for the entire family. A top hat pension scheme. A car for Elizabeth as well as mine. City parking. The kids schooling. Credit cards. Hefty bonuses. You name it.'

'But you weren't happy?'

'It wasn't us,' Edward said for the third time.

It was then Elizabeth also repeated herself.

'The grinding of teeth,' she reminded Edward.

'Oh yes.' He briskly put away the picture. 'I went to our dentist in Sevenoaks. A routine visit. Nothing wrong apart from an odd remark of his. The dentist informed me I was grinding away my teeth. Wearing them right down. Well I went home and told Elizabeth who said she often heard me doing so – in my sleep.'

'And that triggered you,' I said, 'to change your life style?'

Edward and Elizabeth Spinks nodded.

'Yes,' he confirmed. 'We started asking around and following up adverts at weekends.'

'We wanted a complete break,' explained Elizabeth. 'Like a little business of our own. Preferably in the country. To cut out Edward's journeys to the City and back.'

'I remember those,' I said. 'They were dreadful.'

'We soon found,' Edward went on, 'how the whole of Kent and Sussex – indeed the entire Home Counties –

seemed full of people like ourselves wanting to get out of the rat race. So we decided to try further afield. Elizabeth's sister would look after David and Jane at the weekends while we continued our search. The West Country appealed to us, as we used to have our holidays there, but once again suitable small businesses were being snapped up at ridiculously high prices.'

'How did you find this place?'

'By word of mouth. The adverts were never what they seemed and the agents hopeless.'

'I found the same with agents.'

'Hopeless,' Edward nodded. 'It was Elizabeth's sister's husband's brother in the grocery supply trade, who told us about Severnham. The couple owning the store were getting on and wished to retire. We came here the next weekend . . . '

'And fell for it,' said Elizabeth.

'Negotiations followed, but not a lot. The asking price was within our range and, while improvements were needed, we could see the potential. The previous owner and I shook hands on the deal and all went through quite quickly.'

'What did Sir Tim say?' I wanted to know.

'He thought I was mad. Did his best to try and talk me out of it. Why did I want to throw away a comfortable career? Why did I wish to cut myself off from the centre of the world – the City? Why was I leaving him in the lurch?'

'How did the others react?'

'Some of their views were intriguing. The man I liked the least – the smart arse accountant – confided in me. You're well away from here, he said. One day Tim is going to do a deal too far. When the shit hits the fan, you'd be the fall guy.'

'An interesting set of metaphors,' Elizabeth commented. 'More coffee?'

'After that,' Edward continued, 'it was all systems go. We had a month in which to move house, change schools for the kids and take over the running of this business. Funnily enough, the parts I thought would be the hardest proved the best. I like getting up early in the morning and moving around the district when everyone is still in bed. I like my customers, even the difficult ones. Regard them as challenges. As for paperwork, I don't wish to boast, but I am rather good at it.'

'When he gets bogged down,' Elizabeth remarked, 'I sort things out for him.'

'So now you know all about us,' Edward Spinks beamed at me. 'How we came from Sevenoaks to Severnham.'

'What about the grinding of teeth?'

'Stopped doing that from day one down here.'

'Even when he's asleep,' his wife confirmed.

There was a full moon that night. On leaving the Spinks place, I crossed Severnham High Street to look back at the store. Bright moonlight shone on the Cotswold stone frontage, the bay windows, the archway into the cloister-type garden and the fields beyond.

'Been wining and dining?' Oakshott of the Yard appeared at my elbow.

'Hello Stan. Caught me, have you?'

'Oh ah,' he grinned. 'If any of the Spinks silver spoons go missing, I'll know where to look.'

I must move on a few years in order to round off this story. The Spinks continued to succeed in their quiet way. They made progressive changes, all of which enhanced Severnham life. Three examples will suffice.

When Matilda Fluke, who ran the old village post office retired, Edward took over and moved it into his store. He employed her niece Vera to manage that section. Although a simple country girl, Vera soon mastered the thousand or more transactions required of a post office. More important, there was not a penny wrong at the end of each working day.

Shortly afterwards, Vera's two brothers – Fred and Des offered to look after the paper and magazine side. It relieved Edward from getting up at the crack of dawn. It also meant the rest of us receiving our morning and evening papers as if we were living in the heart of the metropolis.

Then Vera's younger sister Kate, who was keen on cooking, started a delicatessen section in the store. This proved highly popular and the most successful of all Edward's enterprises. It allowed him and Elizabeth to take a month off each winter. When the rest of us were enduring Severn Vale weather, we would envy the Spinks their stay in the Bahamas or Azores.

These were but three of the benefits brought by Edward and Elizabeth Spinks to Severnham. There was more to come as I will now relate. It stemmed from what happened in turn to the Spinks children – David and Jane.

David's love of animals led him to become a vet. He went to Liverpool University and, upon obtaining his degree, came back to practise in Severnham. It was a service the district really required. Apart from household pets, there were the farm animals for miles around. David soon needed an assistant. He used to take in students for part of their training. Later he married one, but that is another story.

His surgery, next to the village library, is always full. I once had to see him while he was working. Owners and their pets filled the large waiting room. There were all kinds of dogs, cats in baskets, rabbits in hutches, hamsters and other furry creatures in cages. When I got to David, he was draining the anal glands of a large dog. It was a job neither he nor the dog liked.

'I've never seen,' I greeted him, 'so many different types of animals as in your waiting room.'

'A doctor,' he said, 'only has to look after the human animal while we vets have the rest.' David continued with his task.

'You're always so calm and collected, David,' I said. 'Why, if I walked in here with a baby dinosaur on a lead, I don't think you'd bat an eyelid.'

'Dinosaurs would be interesting.' David threw away the soiled tissues and peeled off his surgical gloves. 'At least they didn't have anal glands.'

As for Jane, she decided in her mid-teens that a show jumping career leading to an Olympic gold medal might be aiming too high. Instead Jane trained at nearby Usk to become a farm secretary. On her return to Severnham, she sent out a direct mail shot to every farmer in the district and duly received an encouraging number of interested replies.

All too soon Jane was visiting the local farms, first in a hatchback then a four-wheel drive. Like the rest of the Spinks, she was trusted – even by secretive Gloucestershire farmers. They came to rely on her getting their books straight and keeping them that way.

Jane would drive home laden with smoked hams,

sides of bacon, clotted cream and a host of other farm foods. Often, because her father's store was already a cornucopia, Jane stopped at my cottage to unload some of the goodies. Most she gave to those really needing it.

Eventually Jane began going out with Geoff Clements who had taken over the 1200 acre family farm. One evening, as she handed me a large Double Gloucester cheese, I noticed the engagement ring which confirmed what I had heard.

'Will you continue the farm secretary work?' I asked.

'Yes, but only for Geoff,' she smiled.

'Lucky man.'

'You will come to our wedding I hope? Father says it's going to be one which Severnham will remember.'

When Edward Spinks told me how, apart from relatives and friends, he was inviting the whole village, I blinked. In my opinion it was a policy fraught with difficulties though I did not say so. What actually happened was far different from the problems I envisaged.

Edward sent out the usual invitations. In addition he put up notices at his shop, the church lychgate, public library and council office. He need only have told one person for the rest to know about it. Within a day half a dozen people told me. And there were some interesting repercussions.

Hilda Twist came into the shop and gushed for all to hear,

'How utterly kind of you! Jane is such a terribly nice girl. I'm sure she and Geoff Clements will make a fine couple. His farm lies right below us, so we'll be able to keep an eye on them.' Hilda launched into peals of self-satisfied laughter.

Then there was Garnet Fluke representing his tribe.

He saw Edward on the grocer's round, came over to him and said,

'Want to tell you, Mr Spinks, there'll be no freeloading. I've put the word round. No freeloading.'

'I plan to have plenty for everyone,' Edward said, but Garnet was adamant. 'No freeloading.'

As the June day drew near, the ladies of Severnham took over the church for their flower displays. They started at the lychgate and decorated the pathway right up to the porch. After that they began in earnest, smothering the interior.

Preparations at the church were nothing compared to those around the Spinks' place. The garden and fields behind it were transformed by marquees, tents, towers and bowers, flags and coloured lights, a band stand, beer hall and car park. Geoff Clements contributed as did the farmers Jane had helped. Food, drinks, presents and offers of help arrived in what seemed like a never-ending stream. Everyone became involved.

Came the day and the weather was perfect. There had been a slight shower the night before cleaning the air. The fields surrounding Severnham shone, the river gleamed, the distant Cotswold and Malvern Hills looked as if they were on the other side of the nearest hedge. It was a perfect day for photography as well as a wedding.

Jane and her father arrived at the church gate in a pony and trap. The crowds there cheered when they saw her. They cheered again when she reappeared after the wedding service. There was not a long photo session as pictures were being taken by a dozen photographer friends all along the way.

The way from the church to the reception was by a cleared footpath to the Spinks' garden. Village children lined it and friends of Jane brought their horses to nod approval as she and Geoff passed. Then it was into the reception with everyone following. There could have been a crush yet, without any rules being laid down, the guests sorted themselves out. Family and friends occupied the main marquee, the rest sat around.

As everyone was settling down for the wedding feast, Sir Tim Bulston put in an appearance. Edward had forgotten about him in the excitement and, before telling what transpired, I should mention how Bulston came to be there in the first place.

Edward and Bulston used to exchange Christmas cards. Sir Tim had seen the wedding announcement in a newspaper and, out of the blue, sent the couple a magnificent present. It consisted of a cut-glass decanter, six matching sherry glasses and a solid silver tray – all from Harrods.

On receipt of this gift, Edward rang his former Chairman and, in the course of their conversation, invited Sir Tim and Lady Bulston to the wedding. To Edward's surprise, Bulston said he might well take up the offer. Then on the evening before the ceremony, Sir Tim rang from the Greenway Hotel near Cheltenham.

'Could you tell me,' he asked, 'how to find this Severnham of yours? It looks mighty complicated on a map.'

'It's even more complicated in reality,' Edward laughed before giving full instructions.

Two seats reserved in the church remained empty and the Bulstons were forgotten until a dark blue Rolls-Royce drew up outside Spinks Stores. Sir Tim looked impressive in his morning suit and the young lady with him truly fabulous. She wore a feathery pink hat with matching outfit, the skirt cut short to display long, slender and seemingly endless legs. Everyone stopped talking and turned to stare at the newcomers.

'Glad you made it.' Edward hurried out to welcome Sir Tim.

'Those lanes.' Bulston looked annoyed. 'They're a maze.'

'Sorry about that. At least you're here and very welcome. And this,' Edward turned to the girl, 'is this Zelda?'

'I'm Candy,' said the girl with a rippling laugh. 'Not Zelda, am I Timmy?'

'Certainly not,' Bulston agreed.

'Come on in.' Edward led them into the main marquee where guests were looking at the name places. 'Let me introduce you to the happy couple and a few of our local friends.'

Of course Conrad and Hilda Twist fastened on to Bulston like leeches.

'I'm going to break this up,' Elizabeth whispered to me. She did so by swapping round names at the tables. The Twists were put with their neighbours. Candy was removed to a separate table among a group of young bachelor farmers. Sir Tim sat next to me.

'I believe,' he said in a sort of growl, 'you were with Thornton Hodges.'

'Still am,' I replied. 'I run their Cheltenham office.'

'Didn't know they had one.' Sir Tim frowned making me regret imparting the information. He was a powerful man who could pick up a telephone and acquire a company quicker than that. At least his proximity allowed me to have a good look at a famous City figure.

Sir Tim Bulston could be described as past his prime.

The thinning hair, brushed over his forehead, was damp with sweat which oozed out of waxen skin. His eyes were dull as one sees in old dogs. The superior smile was fixed, but more sweat appeared under the heavy chin and round the thick neck.

I thought we would have a difficult time with him. Luckily the Meads sat opposite and helped to lighten our table talk. The excellent champagne lifted it all the more and, as the feast continued, Sir Tim became affable and relaxed. He did not seem to mind the rippling laughter from Candy who was enjoying herself with the bachelor farmers.

What went on at that table – and afterwards during the dancing – soon became common knowledge in the village. The young bachelor farmers included Laurie Palmer, son of Tiny, who was even taller and pushier than his father. Laurie had an enviable reputation with the girls and his friends egged him on to take advantage of this opportunity.

'Y'know summat,' he informed the sophisticated Londoner, 'we'd make a great pair.'

'Do you think so?' she teased him.

'Know so,' Laurie replied. 'Teach you a thing or two.'

'Could you put a bull to a cow?' one wag wanted to know.

'I'm quick at picking up techniques,' Candy replied, 'once someone shows me how to do them.' Roars of laughter from the young farmers' table kept interrupting the best man's speech.

Many tales were told of Laurie's progress with Candy, but the two best incidents should paint the picture. After the meal Laurie asked her to dance and Candy agreed. As they gyrated madly he said to her,

'I realise you're going with that old feller, but you're the most gorgeous girl I'll ever see in the whole of my life. Is there any chance of you coming round the back of the barn with me?' Laurie Palmer had been hoping for a kiss perhaps so her reply shook him.

'Why not?' she said. 'Only you mustn't get too carried away. If you knew how much this outfit cost old Timmy.'

Thus Laurie did achieve his original goal and later the others asked what she kissed like. His description amused the whole of Severnham. I am not betraying a love secret if I repeat what Laurie said of Candy's kissing ability.

'She had,' his eyes rolled, 'a tongue like a tin opener.'

Meanwhile the rest of us carried on with the wedding feast's tamer delights and Sir Tim had a long talk with the Spinks. He eventually noticed Candy's absence and later her reappearance without much surprise.

'I've had such fun,' she said quite openly. 'Thanks for bringing me here, Timmykins.'

'We have to go back to London,' he announced, again with no rancour. We noted Candy never said it in as many words, but she made it plain he was fortunate to have her.

While Candy went inside with Elizabeth to get ready for her journey back to London, Edward and Sir Tim talked as they waited. Then Edward, in his capacity as host, was called away and Bulston turning to me remarked,

'What a waste.'

'Pardon?'

'Spinks. Down here. He could have gone far in the

City. People liked him. Admired him. His cheerfulness.
Integrity. Commonsense.'

'Edward is very popular here.'

'He was well thought of where it counts.' Sir Tim
showed he did not like interruptions. 'I came wondering
if he might have tired of country life, but it is evident he
prefers to be a big fish in a small pond. Tragic really.'

I could not help asking Sir Tim Bulston what he
meant – deferentially of course. He said,

'The Americans have a good name for such a person.
It is under-achiever.'

Dottie's Angel

The Severnham District Council is an enthusiastic expo-
nent of two golden rules followed by most other uncivil
services. If the matter is a trivial one – such as relaying a
few paving stones or shifting a minor street sign – then
it gets the full treatment. There are meetings, discus-
sions and consultations; plans, notices and releases to
the local press. If on the other hand the subject is so
important it affects the whole community then the
highest security prevails. There are meetings, but these
are without agendas or minutes. All members are sworn
to secrecy. Should anyone outside the closed circle
manage to find out what is happening, this is indignantly
denied. Use of the expression, 'There is absolutely no

truth whatsoever in the rumour,' means it is certain to take place.

Such was the case of Operation Opportunity, in itself a misnomer. The whole business stemmed from what to do with the Manor House at Lesser Sodham. At one time it had been the home of a then wealthy local family. The surviving couple, elderly and impoverished, had retired to live in the lodge while the manor became a mental home for the simple minded rather than the dangerous. Care in the Community, another misnomer, shifted those patients out to wander city streets. The council then had to find further use for the extensive building. What they came up with needs to be explained before my story begins.

Certain bodies connected with the Home Office, Prison and Probation Services wished to have somewhere for 'an exciting new treatment of young offenders'. The general idea was to indulge rather than punish and included long holidays to exotic places. Once this principle had been established, it was decided those going to such centres should not be local lads. They had to be taken out of their environment which meant offenders from, say, Gloucestershire going to Shropshire and those from Birmingham coming to Lesser Sodham. Large sums of money were involved and Conrad Twist rubbed his hands at the increase to his budget.

When workmen began refurbishing the Manor House, fitting out fifty rooms with central heating, double glazing and en suite facilities, questions were asked. What is happening? Who will be occupying the rooms? Rumours had it they would be drug addicts then rapists. These were vigorously denied. After that came the report of a centre for young Birmingham offenders.

That too was shrugged off as ridiculous. The council stuck to its denials until the coachloads arrived.

Gradually, reluctantly the truth emerged. Severnham was to have fifty hard cases from Birmingham. However there was no need to worry. The attendees, as they were called, would be attended by tough ex-army sergeants and the whole establishment managed by an expert in these matters. His name was Becker and he appeared at a press conference with Chief Councillor Twist to assure the rest of us no one would be affected.

The first people to be affected were the couple living in the lodge. Shortly after the coaches arrived, some of the lads strolled down the drive. The lodge interested them and the newcomers walked round it peering through the windows. The old couple were having a meal and the man came out.

'Clear off!' he shouted and the youngsters cleared off. Next morning the flower beds and kitchen garden to the lodge were found wrecked.

The old man went straight to the house, which his family once owned, to complain. He saw a warden and was taken to Mr Becker. If such a personality is possible, the chief warden looked like an amiable Adolf Hitler. He had dark hair falling over his forehead, a little moustache and he walked jerkily. His eyes were fanatical, especially in defence of his boys.

'You did what?' Becker exclaimed. 'You told them to clear off? But this is their home now, Mr . . . I didn't catch your name. Many of them never had proper homes. I and my colleagues have been trying to tell them they are getting a home yet, when they arrive here on their first morning, you say clear off. You are not making it easy for me, Mr . . . Oh, dearie me no.'

Lower Severnham lies halfway between Lesser Sodham and our village. The midway mark has a yuppie
housing estate. There, as is the lifestyle of yuppies, both
partners go out to work. If any children 'slip past the net'
so to speak, these are handed over to grandmothers.
Therefore yuppie houses are prone to stay empty during
the day. They are also stuffed full of electronic goodies –
television sets, video recorders, computers and the
like – which have a certain attraction for young burglars.
No sooner were the lads installed at Lesser Sodham
Manor House than there followed a series of Lower
Severnham break-ins.

Break-in might not be the best description. The lads
would go for nice healthy country walks and come upon
a house with a back door lock which could be opened
far too easily. Once inside a swift glance told them what
was saleable. They would then use a nearby car to take
their spoils into town for quick disposal and hard cash.
More often than not the car was brought back to its
parking lot and the back door of the house left locked
for the owner's return.

When our PC Stan Oakshott went to see the chief
warden the latter indignantly asked,

'Where is your proof, Constable . . . ? Just because we
are at Lesser Sodham you want to give my lads a bad
name.'

'Two of them were seen, Mr Becker.'

'Call me Ray. Seen by whom? Were they my lads?
Others are obviously taking advantage because we are
here. Even if two of my lads were involved, which I
doubt, it's a lengthy process. A long and difficult exercise weaning them from their former ways. I and the
Home Office expect the police to co-operate. We are

conducting an important experiment here, Constable whatever you're called . . . Changing youngsters' lives for the better.'

Next the problems spread to Severnham Village. The first of two locks on Edward's liquor store was forced. A computer went missing from Chris Fluke's workshop. The Restoration was broken into on three occasions. I nearly suffered.

I returned home one afternoon from Cheltenham and found a couple of Lesser Sodham lads in my front garden.

'What are you doing here?' I wanted to know.

'Just looking,' one of them said and the other added, 'An interesting place you've got.'

'Out,' I said opening the front gate.

After they drifted through the gate and I had shut it, the older of the two remarked,

'We looked in your window. You haven't got a video recorder.'

'No.'

'I could get you one for a hundred quid.'

'I don't want it.'

'A Megasonic worth three ninety-nine.' He looked at his companion. 'Ninety quid then. I'm giving it away.'

'Not to me,' I said.

The two lads glanced at each other, shrugged and set off along the lane. They tried the church, but fortunately four parishioners were inside doing the flowers. The village women looked so formidable and spoke so forcibly that the two lads left without a word.

A week later one of the lads attempted to steal a child's bike from the side of Basher Fluke's bungalow.

He was reaching for it when a huge paw of a hand grasped his collar and lifted him into the air.

'What do you think you're doing?' Basher enquired.

The lad could not answer because of semi-strangulation and justifiable fear.

'Listen to me,' Basher shook him. 'Don't you come sneaking round here again. Trying to steal things. I know all about you lot. If I see or hear of you – any of you – I'll be after the culprit. Straight out to the Manor House. Straight through the wall if need be. So watch it!'

A minute later the lad was seen running away from Basher's place. Although the boy did not want to talk about what had happened, Chief Warden Becker got the whole story out of him. How he had stopped to ask for a glass of water and how this big man had responded by hitting him. A formal complaint was made against Basher Fluke. PC Stan Oakshott tried to smooth over the matter, but it went through higher channels and Basher ended up in a magistrates' court.

'You ought to be ashamed of yourself,' said the magistrate. 'We are doing all we can to reclaim these unfortunate boys and you set them a bad example. You are hereby fined £100 plus £35 costs for a most serious offence. I must also warn you, if you persist with your bad behaviour, you will go to prison.'

There were some interesting repercussions to the Basher Fluke incident. Two of the wardens called at his bungalow with a crate of beer. While commiserating with him – and sharing the cans – they told him how frustrated they were with the Manor House regime.

'It ain't even a regime,' said one.

'We can't lay a finger on them,' said the other.

'We was in the Army.'

'Made men into soldiers.'

'But not this lot.'

'Do as they please.'

About ten days later, the wardens and young inmates all disappeared from Lesser Sodham. At first we believed they had left for good, but the truth was . . . well, unbelievable. They had gone, with special funding from the Home Office, for a cruise of the Norwegian fjords. We heard how Basher and the Flukes at The Piggy almost cried into their beer.

About a fortnight later I happened to meet the two lads who had been in my garden. They wanted to know whether I was still in the market for a video recorder. I changed the subject to their recent holiday and they said,

'Dead boring it was.'

'Nothing but sea and them bloody cliffs.'

'A wonderful opportunity for you,' I said.

'Yeah,' they conceded. 'The grub wasn't bad.'

The next repercussion was a meeting called by the council to tell the rest of us what Operation Opportunity was meant to achieve. Chief Councillor Conrad Twist no less chaired the meeting and Chief Warden Ray Becker addressed a full audience. In the case of Twist, he kept his feet firmly in both camps. While welcoming all contributions to council funds, he fully appreciated the fears of the local electorate. In the case of Becker, the chief warden waxed lyrical about the value of such work. His ending was particularly upbeat.

'You must appreciate,' Becker told us, 'that these poor unfortunate lads either come from broken homes or no homes at all. Their infant years have been rotten. Many were hurt or abused by a succession of so-called parents and even foster parents. They are not guilty. We are guilty for allowing such a shocking state of affairs to exist. We are all guilty. Thank you for your time, ladies and gentlemen. Thank you,' he turned to Conrad Twist, 'Mr er . . . Thank you.'

Afterwards there was coffee and circulation. I met Dottie Mead. Before I could say a word, the vicar's wife told me,

'That man is absolutely right. The history of recidivism is an appalling one.'

'Of what?' I ventured.

'Crime and punishment. All those ghastly prisons, tortures and floggings. It is wonderful to meet a man who is bold enough to try and put an end to it.'

Inevitably Dottie had to have a word with Becker. She greeted him like a messiah and he assumed the mantle of Adolf Hitler meeting a pure Aryan. Presently Conrad Twist and a reporter from the local rag joined us.

'I am proud,' Twist said, 'to lead an innovative council.' He gave the reporter a quote-unquote nod. Meanwhile Dottie and Becker were enlarging on their mutual interests. She said,

'You are an inspiration to us all, Mr Becker.'

'Please call me Ray.'

'I'd be happy to, Ray. I'm the vicar's wife, Dorothy Mead. You did uplift me.'

'Glad to hear that, Miss . . . ' Becker responded. 'But it's not easy. My boys will be . . . er, boys.'

'One has to make allowances,' Dottie nodded. 'Don't you agree, Mr Twist?'

'Of course I do, Mrs Mead.' Conrad eyes flickered towards the reporter whose ball point pen was poised over his notepad.

79

'A broad canvas I always say.' I watched the press man look puzzled as he wrote 'broad canvas'.

'You must,' Becker said to Dottie, 'come and see what we try to do at the Manor House.'

'Delighted,' Dottie responded. 'I once spoke on the side of your cause, Ray. At the Oxford Union.'

'Did you now,' Becker was clearly impressed. 'Then you will have to visit us, Miss . . . '

It was arranged that a small party would visit the Manor House at Lesser Sodham on the following Saturday morning. Our Chief Councillor was enthusiastic during the announcement (in front of reporters) but never went. However it gave those of us who did go a chance to see for ourselves and meet the inmates.

The Manor House had been transformed. The rooms were clean and warm; the games hall spacious and well equipped; the food planned and served by catering experts. We were allowed to look everywhere. Each boy had his own room and was free to decorate it as he wished. Posters and pictures were – well, colourful. The latest videos stood neatly lined up next to the latest television sets. Hi-fi and computers littered the place.

While Dottie enthused, I talked to the two wardens who had treated Basher Fluke after the bicycle incident.

'Your charges do all right,' I remarked to them.

'You can say that again.'

'What happens if you get one who's really difficult?'

'Wouldn't happen here,' both men assured me.

'Why not?'

'It's cushy and they're crafty. If one of them tried to push it too far the others would do him. See that fair haired lad over there. That's Angel. Not his real name. He's called Angel 'cause he seems so angelic. He's the worst of the bunch. Doesn't look as if butter would melt in his mouth, but he's a real villain. No good. Never will be.'

The next move in Operation Opportunity was a large notice outside the council office. It said that, in order to integrate trainees at Lesser Sodham into the Severnham community, people were invited to assist with their education programme. Help would be voluntary and unpaid. The notice was signed by a minor official which meant Conrad Twist was distancing himself from the project.

Dottie was the only person who volunteered. She came round to see me, indignant at the lack of response.

'You will join as well? Won't you?'

'Sorry Dottie. I work a full time day.'

'If we all made excuses, nothing would ever get done.'

'If the Home Office, Probation and Prison Services want to educate the boys, there should be proper funding.'

'It's money then, is it?' Dottie asked, tartly for her.

'As a matter of fact, yes,' I told her. 'Not so much for me, but for qualified people trying to make a living. That place must have cost a bomb. Now they want unpaid labour.'

'They shall have my services,' said Dottie. 'I was only telling Andy the other day how market forces have become a modern heresy. I suggested he should preach a sermon on it.'

'Is he going to?'

'He had an engine gearbox problem at the time. You men.' Dottie rose to leave. 'You keep avoiding the real issues in life. Like practical Christianity.'

This was the nearest Dottie and I ever came to having a row. We both felt guilty and tried to make amends – Dottie by relating her contributions to Operation Opportunity and me by listening to them. She said,

'I'm giving lessons twice a week in Creative Writing. It is a psychological ploy. Getting them to unburden themselves. To remove their inhibitions. Reveal innermost thoughts.'

'Are you succeeding?'

'It's early days yet, but most interesting.'

'In what way?'

'There's a lad there who looks like an angel . . . '

'Yes, Dottie. One of the wardens told me his nickname is Angel.'

'That's right. He has been most helpful. Comes to my classes. Listens carefully. Makes sure the others do the same.'

'That's good,' I said. 'When you are giving these classes, is there a warden present?'

'Yes. Why? He doesn't take part. Sits at the back of the room looking bored. The wardens are old army deadbeats.'

'Not a very Christian attitude, Dottie.'

'Point taken.' She nodded. 'But I was telling you about Angel. I think I am getting through to him. Or perhaps starting to understand him. I asked the class to try writing a short story and he came up with this. It's supposed to be Science Fiction and yet . . . What do you think of it?'

The story was not long and it had been written in capital letters. Its title was 'I am Vardak'.

'I am Vardak. I live on a planet called Destroy. It's called Destroy cause all its inhabitants are Destroyers.

This makes it tough on me cause we are all the same and cancel (spelt kancel) each other out. You can't get anywhere on Destroy without hassle (spelt hassel). So I made myself a star ship and went off to explore the universe. It's a dangerous place the universe full of aliens so all I got was more hassle (spelt hasel). Then I found Planet Earth. It looked a nice place from space blue and green with white clouds. I landed near Brum and found life there dead easy cause I was tougher than everyone else on Earth. I could punch holes through people and knock their heads off if I liked. I had blasters as well and plenty of ammo. I began to like Earth cause I was the most powerfulest person of all. Signed Vardak.'

'Wow!' I said, then quoted, 'The most powerfulest person of all'.

'What wrong with the phrase?' Dottie was clearly annoyed by my attitude. 'A triple superlative. Shakespeare used them. The most unkindest cut of all. *Julius Caesar.*'

'Point taken.' This time I nodded.

'But what do you think?'

'I think Angel has a huge chip on his shoulder. Could be a dangerous one. You should watch out.'

I must say this for Dottie, she persisted. Every Tuesday and Thursday afternoon, she went along to the Manor House at Lesser Sodham and gave lessons. She invited the lads to mix with the local community and even try going to church. Neither did happen. There was too much of a gap.

'I'm afraid there is,' Dottie told me. 'How can anyone make up for those negative formative years in a few weeks? One can only try. Must keep on trying.'

So she persisted. The rest of us watched, but did little

or nothing. We either thought the whole matter a waste of time or, at the best, mutely wished Dottie some little success.

During the next three months, there were more incidents involving the young offenders, also some changeovers. Half a dozen or so left and were replaced by others from Birmingham. By all accounts that city had an inexhaustible supply. However Angel remained the focus of Dottie's attention and she felt at last the treatment was getting through to him.

'You should join me on one of my afternoons,' she said, 'and see for yourself.'

I made excuses – my work in Cheltenham, working at home – but Dottie can be persuasive. To please her, I agreed to go. I walked round to the vicarage and there was Dottie waiting by her hatchback. She said,

'I had a feeling you'd put it off at the last minute.'

'No. Here I am.'

Dottie chatted as she drove, negotiating the twisty lanes between Severnham and Lesser Sodham.

'They are bored,' she told me. 'Bored out of their minds. The lads have so much energy, but it is not being channelled anywhere either to their or the country's advantage. We seem to concentrate on penalties for crimes while ignoring the causes.'

At the Manor House, she parked the hatchback in a new car park by the side. I held her books and gazed around. There were boys hoeing flowerbeds and one with a motor mower going up and down the long lawn. Dottie came over to me and took the books saying,

'This way. We're a little late.'

Her class waited in a room at the end of a corridor. There were about ten pupils and a warden sat just inside the door. Angel, I noticed, was in the front row. I decided to sit beside the warden who I had previously met. He gave me a wary smile.

'I've been through your latest stories,' Dottie told her class, 'and there are some definite improvements. Especially with you Angel.'

'Especially with him,' one of the lads sneered and the others guffawed.

'Seriously,' said Dottie, 'you've all done jolly well. I am now going to deal with each in turn, telling you your strengths and weaknesses. Let me start with Barry Tewson.' She opened the top exercise book.

The session was a ninety-minute one with a tea break in the middle. During the break the warden asked me what I thought and I countered by asking him back,

'What do you think? You're the expert.'

'No expert,' he admitted. 'It's a job and the money's not bad.' The ex-army man sipped his tea then said, 'Angel's taking a lot of stick from the rest. Teacher's boy. People should remember the driving force behind these lads is anti-authority. They don't – won't – side with authority.'

'Mrs Mead is not authority.'

'I know that and you know that. To the boys however she's part of authority.'

'Are you saying there's any danger?'

'I wouldn't think so,' the warden replied. 'Mrs Mead is acceptable. But if one of the lads, like that Angel, is pushed, you never know what will happen.'

I was to remember his words when something did happen three quarters of an hour later.

The class over, Dottie and I said goodbye to the lads and went to the car park. I had again taken Dottie's books while she looked into her bag for the keys. Suddenly Dottie cried,

'Oh no! Look what I've done. Left them in the ignition and locked the doors.'

'Have you a spare key?'

'No. Andy lost that. Fortunately, I'm a member of the RAC. I'll go to Mr Becker's office and phone for their assistance.'

I followed her and we found Ray Becker drinking tea. He had his own tray with a silver-plated tea pot and bone china.

'There's no need to ring anyone, Miss, er . . . You forget we have specialists here. Getting into cars I mean.' He pressed a button on his intercom and said to someone, 'Have Angel come to my office.'

When Angel arrived his blue eyes were bright and his smile ready, but the face remained a blank.

'Ah Angel,' Becker greeted him. 'Here's a chance to show what you can do. Miss, er . . . has locked the keys in her car. Be a good lad and get them for her.'

'Yes Sir,' said Angel is a curiously neutral voice.

'I'll come with you,' Dottie half rose until Becker waved her back into the chair.

'No, no, no. Can't have you witnessing the tricks of the trade. Can we, Angel?'

'No Sir,' said Angel. 'May I go now, Sir?'

'Certainly. Off you go. As quickly as you can.'

Angel left and Becker half-offered us tea.

'You probably had some during the break . . . ?'

'Yes, we did,' said Dottie.

'Anyway, Angel'll be back in no time. The lads reckon they can open any car door within three seconds. There you are . . . '

Angel knocked and entered with Dottie's car keys.

'That was incredible!' Dottie said as she and I went along the corridor. She had thanked Mr Becker and particularly Angel.

We came out of the front entrance and turned towards the car park at the side. Several lads were standing around, but they became busy as we passed them. Their behaviour seemed to be peculiar and I was thinking about this when Dottie's voice interrupted my thoughts. Again she cried,

'Oh no!'

I turned to look at her then the car. The windscreen had been smashed and a heavy stone lay on the front seat. There was broken glass everywhere.

'I suppose,' I said, 'we'll have to go back and see Mr Becker about this.'

She shook her head.

'I hope you don't mind. It's a warm day. I intend to drive the car as it is.'

This is what Dottie did. She removed the stone, got into the car and started the engine. We crunched along the gravel, past staring boys. At the end of the driveway, we turned towards Severnham. By then tears were running down Dottie's cheeks, but she kept on driving.

At the vicarage I made her tea and asked what she was going to do.

'Nothing,' Dottie answered. 'No complaints, but no more lessons.'

I never saw Mr Becker or his boys again so I can only report, at secondhand, what happened next. Andy Mead told me Becker came two days later to apologise and pay for a new windscreen.

'I had already got one from a place I know,' said Andy, 'and fitted it myself.'

'What was Dottie's reaction to Becker's visit?'

'He annoyed her. Kept saying Miss. She told him, I am the vicar's wife and therefore Mrs. She also said it was her fault for leaving the keys in the ignition and his for using Angel. They had quite an argument about it.'

'Mm. What now?'

'All over. She's not going back. He won't trouble her any further. Angel has been sent somewhere else. A tougher regime, Becker kept stressing.'

Dottie did not refer to the matter for a long while. At last, weeks later, there was some news about the establishment at Lesser Sodham and she commented as follows.

'Did you know that, if all the places for young offenders were wide open, 75 percent would chose to stay inside. Most do not have parents, relatives or friends waiting for them. Usually there is no one looking forward to their release. Instead there are only the streets, petty crime, perhaps dope and certainly prisons as they grow older.'

'Tragic,' I had to agree.

What about the Manor House at Lesser Sodham? Well the forces of national government and local politics intervened there.

At the time, some politician seized the opportunity of a party conference to call for tougher action against young offenders. He frothed about 'short sharp shocks' as he would have done about branding irons a few centuries ago. He was wildly applauded and his personal rating soared for a week.

Operation Opportunity was forgotten. Our establishment shut and the boys conveyed elsewhere – to double march before being turned out once again on to city streets.

Their departure from the Manor House was hastened by our chief councillor. He had an idea which would both make more money and enhance his prestige. As Conrad Twist explained it to the local rag,

'The county needs a suitable place to train council staff. A place where they can go, away from the stresses and strains of office, to exchange ideas. A conference centre with full facilities. I am putting it to my fellow chief councillors throughout Gloucestershire.'

Severnham Monster

The Case of the Severnham Monster was to test our PC Stan Oakshott over a long period. Many wild rumours and false pieces of information circulated in the district at the time, so this account is an attempt to set the record straight. Stan favoured me from the start with inside data. To this day he often allows me to buy him a quiet pint or two on the strength of it. Let me therefore begin at the beginning.

It was Saturday morning during high summer when Stan first called about the case. At that stage nothing was public knowledge. There had been certain incidents which Stan kept to himself. Yet I was not surprised when he propped his police bike against my front gate and came up the garden path removing his trouser clips. Stan often called when I was about to drink freshly made coffee, tea or other beverages. I answered the front door with the coffee pot in my free hand.

'Come in, Stan,' I said. 'You must have smelt this.'

'I'm here on business,' he replied, 'but a cup of coffee would be welcome. Been up half the night.'

'Oh? Anything serious?'

'Dunno yet.' Stan sat and sipped at his coffee.

With Stan, as with most of the other villagers, it is best not to rush him. Information has to be given rather than extracted and progress can be slow.

'You have a good view of Severnham Hill from your front windows,' Stan eventually said. 'Specially your study window.'

'Oh ah,' I confirmed in the local manner.

'Have you a telescope or a pair of binoculars?'

'Neither. Why do you ask?'

'Wondered.' Stan stirred his coffee. 'I hoped you might have seen strange goings on.'

'Like what?'

'This is the third summer I've had it.'

'Had what, Stan?'

He helped himself to another spoonful of Demerara sugar before saying,

'The Severnham Monster.'

'A monster? Here at Severnham? You're joking.'

'Maybe. Maybe not. This is the third summer as I said.' Stan drank more coffee then proceeded. 'You might be able to help me – living here with a view of the hill. Happen to see summat going up the hill and entering the wood. Should do as it's all of ten foot tall.'

'Ten foot? You're pulling my leg.'

'Didn't stay up half the night to pull your leg,' Stan sounded hurt. 'I'll tell you about it if you promise to keep mum as well as keep a look out.'

'I'd notice a ten foot monster.'

'That's what I was thinking,' he agreed.

My view of Severnham Hill is of a long rise about a mile across and just over 600 feet high. To the right, on the south west side, there is the lane leading to ten recently built houses. To the left lies the wood going back to medieval times. The trees curve over the crest of the hill and run down in the direction of the main road.

'You get walkers on the hill during the day,' Stan was saying. 'People with their dogs. At night – specially during warm summer ones – the wood is a favourite place for courting couples. Traditional like.'

'Oh ah.'

'Used it myself,' said Stan, 'when me and Jackie were making up our minds.' Jackie Oakshott was the sister of Janis Palmer. Both were jokey girls, always having a laugh at the world in general and the antics of men in particular.

Stan gave a slow smile as if still savouring his courting days. I topped up our coffees before prodding him further.

'Now there's a monster in the wood?'

'So they say. Latest sighting late evening Wednesday.'

'Which took you up there last night?'

'Ah, but I never saw nothing. Serious though, taking a walk in the wood has been a tradition round these parts for hundreds of years. The girls like it, you know. The wildness. The loneliness. Can let themselves go a bit. Maybe all the way. Must maintain tradition.'

I promised Stan to keep a look-out and did so whenever I remembered. A week went by during which the high summer became drier and warmer. Dottie Mead brought me some strawberries and I asked her if there was any history to the Medieval Wood.

'What sort of history?' she asked back.

'Incidents.'

'Let me think.' Dottie did so. 'The Victorian land-owners claimed it was theirs and tried putting gate-keepers in it. A Parliamenterian force is reported to have camped in the wood before ambushing some Royalists. And, oh yes, the chronicles tell of a giant monk who took refuge thereabouts after being thrown out of his monastery for lewd behaviour.'

The last item was interesting, but I will warn the reader it proved to be a red herring. Life is much more complicated than that.

As I say, a week went by. I was crossing The Yard after a check-up by Dr Prosser when Stan appeared at the front door of his police house.

'Spare a minute?'

'Sure.'

'Definite sighting last night. The Monster. Come on in.'

Severnham's police house is larger than it looks. The frontage is narrow, but it goes back a long way. The police part is to the left of the front door. A passage leads to an inner door and the family side of the building.

The inside door was open and Stan's wife Jackie greeted me with a cheerful 'Hi there!' His two sons – midget versions of him – were playing in the passage. Stan steered me left into a police office-cum-interview room. A mug of tea was on the table and Jackie came in with a second for me before I was seated.

'Another sighting,' Stan said when we were alone. 'My sister Nancy. She's been courting one of the Clements' lads for a long time. We hoped there'd be some action when they went up to the wood.'

'This was last night?'

'After midnight. Nearer one in the morning. The warm weather, nearly a full moon and all that. I had said to our Nan if you can't seduce James there you never will. Seems they were getting quite friendly when she saw the Monster.'

'What was it like? Did it see them?'

'Like? Nan said it was black, shaped like a bat and at least ten feet high. The Monster was coming through the woods towards them but, when she gave a yell, it veered off and left them. Seemed to disappear.'

'Did um, James Clements see it?'

'No. He was sort of otherwise engaged at the time. Never saw a thing and wondered what our Nan was on about. But she's a down-to-earth girl. Wouldn't make up anything like that. There is summat in the Medieval Wood.' Stan stood up abruptly and went to a closed door. 'Here's summat else you should know.'

The closed door had a notice stuck to it. The notice read 'Incident Room. Keep Out'. Stan produced keys and opened double locks. He switched on a light because the room had no window.

'Have to keep Jackie and the kids outside,' he explained. 'Wouldn't want confidential police information talked around the district.'

The walls of the room were covered with pinboards to which maps, charts and lists had been fixed. There was a large scale map showing Severnham District and another of the Medieval Wood. The wood map had sprouted coloured pins and little cards giving dates followed by capital letters.

'This was the Monster's first reported sighting,' said Stan. He pointed and read out, 'Three years ago. Twenty-sixth of June. Mr A and Mrs B. Surprised they came and told me.'

'Why were you surprised?'

'Not married to each other. Had a similar one here. Mr E and Mrs F. She was in a state of shock and went to see Doctor Prosser. He sent her to me.' Stan pointed at other cards then to a filing cabinet. 'The identities of all concerned are locked in there.'

'You're impressing me, Stan. Where were Nancy and James when they saw the Monster?'

'On the south side,' said Stan. He indicated a new card labelled Mr X and Miss Y. 'I'm running out of alphabet. About time I took action to catch the culprit.'

'Have you any leads?'

'Hunches more like. Them ten houses were put up four years ago. The sightings began in the following June. They take place during the hot weather and tend to be near them houses.' Stan showed me a list beside the map. It read as follows:-

1 Twist
2 Semple
3 Barter
4 Siviter-Smith
5 Greatorex
6 Farquahar
7 Stallard

8 Patterson
9 Moriarty
10 Dolland

'You think it's one of those?' I asked.

'Just a hunch.'

'My guess is Moriarty.'

'Why him? He's a Professor . . . '

'Of Mathematics?'

'No, of Music. Teaches in Cheltenham. So does his missus. She's a Dame. Why did you pick the old boy?'

'I was being silly. Sherlock Holmes's greatest enemy.'

'Oh ah.' Oakshott of the Yard was not impressed.

'What now, Stan?'

'We've got to catch him before some poor woman has a fatal spasm. The Medieval Wood is all of fifteen acres, so I'll need back-up. There's only me out here. I don't want to bring in the Cheltenham and Gloucester boys. They'd laugh their silly heads off. This is a Severnham job. Would you lend a hand?'

'One must help the law.'

'Too true,' Stan agreed. 'It'll mean you giving up the best part of a night's sleep, mind.'

'When are you thinking of doing it?'

'Friday or Saturday. The glass is steady. The fine hot weather should hold.'

Thus we left it at that. Stan Oakshott said he would either call or drop a note through my letterbox. By Thursday evening I was beginning to wonder if anything had been arranged when Stan phoned instead.

'Everything's fixed up for tomorrow night. Suit you?'

'Yes.'

'We aim to start at ten.'

'Right.'

'Rendezvous at Tiny Palmer's farmhouse. Nearest to the wood, you see.'

'I'll be there. Tiny knows then?'

'Oh ah. There was another sighting last night. The woman ran to the farm. Proper hysterical the Palmers told me.'

It was arranged I wear dark clothing and bring a torch. During that Friday at work, I became increasingly excited by the promise of adventure. Stan said he had a plan. According to him all the details were worked out. The Monster – or whoever it was – would in his words 'Be suitably apprehended'.

On getting back to the cottage, I had a shower, put on my dark grey gardening trousers and shirt, then cooked myself a meal. I even had time to fit new torchlight batteries. This took me until six so there was only another four hours to wait before the operation was due to start.

At last, at a quarter to ten, I set out for Tiny Palmer's farmhouse. There had been a lovely sunset and now, from the east, night was curving over the sky like a deep blue coverlet.

Instead of approaching the farmhouse along the lanes, I cut across Tiny's fields. This was foolish of me because I had to make a diversion in order to avoid a prize bull. I was late and approaching the farmhouse at a trot when I saw several cars there. It had not occurred to me until then that Stan would be using other people.

The other people were Stan's wife Jackie, Tiny and Janis Palmer, Dr and Mrs Prosser, the dentist and his wife Ruby, also Miss Nook the junior school teacher. All were dressed in dark clothing and carrying torches.

'Sorry I'm late,' I mumbled my apologies.

'We nearly started without you,' Stan said severely.

'Coffee?' said Janis Palmer handing me a mug. There was a strange smell to it. When I sniffed she explained, 'Brandy. To keep out the cold.'

As the night was a hot one, I wondered. The coffee seemed to be made of brandy. What Janis went on to say, made me wonder all the more.

'I'm glad you made it. We are going to play the parts of courting couples. Miss Nook thought she'd be left without a partner.'

This latest snippet of information demanded a cheery wave across the room at Miss Nook. Although the teacher looked frail and wore thick glasses, she enjoyed a certain reputation. The night might well be different from that which I had anticipated.

'Ahem!' Oakshott of the Yard gave us an official cough. 'Seeing as how we're late already, I'd better get on with it. The five couples slip out of here at ten minute intervals to take up strategic positions like in the wood.'

'What kind are those?' Ruby asked, causing Janis and Jackie to hoot with laughter.

'Jackie and I,' Stan ignored her, 'leave first and go to the centre of the wood. After that Tiny and Janis will make for the north side, Dr and Mrs Prosser the south, our dentist friends east and the last two west. There the couples can either patrol or lie low on look out.'

'Look out,' Ruby repeated, rolling her eyes suggestively.

'I see you've all brought torches,' Stan continued. 'They should not be used during the first part of the operation. I'm convinced the alleged monster is some nutter who goes up there to frighten people. So I want him to get well into the wood before we act. Here.' He handed a police whistle to each of the men. 'When the monster's past you and towards me, start blowing and flashing.'

'Wow!' Ruby shrieked. 'It looks like being quite a night.'

'Right then,' Stan said briskly. 'Any questions or ideas before Jackie and I get underway?'

'It's a good plan, Stan,' Ruby said, 'But I should like to suggest one small improvement. It's going to be deadly dull spending a night in the wood with one's own partner. We should change over to keep us fully alert. And here is my choice.' Ruby strode across the room and gripped my arm.

Before I, or anyone else for that matter, could think of what to say next, her husband dentist approached Miss Nook.

'I do hope,' he enquired with a mixture of gallantry and lechery, 'you will do me the honour?'

'Anything,' Miss Nook blinked. 'Anything.'

'In that case, Jackie,' Janis called, 'I'll take Stan off your hands.'

'And I'll look after Tiny.' Both hooted at the switch.

Which left Dr and Mrs Prosser.

'Hm,' he frowned. 'We'll remain as we are, thank you.'

Before we left the farmhouse in our readjusted pairs, a further surprise awaited us. Janis Palmer had assembled five generous hip flasks of brandy to help each couple through the night. Ruby, who had one hand locked on my upper arm, grabbed the biggest flask with the other and shoved it in the pocket of her jacket.

99

'Come on,' she whispered fiercely before we had even left the farmyard, 'We're supposed to be courting.' Ruby shifted her grip to round my waist.

Our path led upwards towards the west side of the wood, which was also the end nearest to the ten houses. There were hardly any lights to be seen, probably due to their well-made curtains. One of the houses had an open garage and, as we climbed, a car came along and turned into it.

'No 4,' I remarked. 'Siviter-Smith.'

'What are you on about?' Ruby asked.

'The car went into No 4. The Siviter-Smiths live there. He's a financial consultant.'

'My, you are knowledgeable about such things.' There was a significant pause, then Ruby said, 'Stan's sure it'll be one of them lot. What do you think?'

'My money's on No. 9. A Professor Moriarty. Bound to be. Sherlock Holmes's enemy.'

'Yeah, well,' Ruby let me help her over a stile, 'Whoever it is must be kinky. Know what I mean?'

Since leaving the farmhouse, we had not seen any of the others. We seemed to be alone as the dark medieval wood loomed ahead of us. There was nearly a full moon silvering the hills, but casting deep shadows. A nightjar sounded and was answered by an owl. Some distance away, a fox laughed.

'Glad I'm not by myself.' Ruby shivered. 'Do you mind if I have a tot?'

'Help yourself,' I said and she did.

Strangely enough it was not so scary once we entered the wood. Our eyes quickly adjusted to the gloom which was relieved by the moonlight. We went about fifty

yards between the great beech tree trunks before paus-
ing and looking around.

'What now, darling?' Ruby enquired.

'Um . . . '

'Do we stand up or lie down?'

'Let's wander round a bit.'

'OK. Find a comfortable spot.'

It was obvious Ruby had one objective in mind. We
walked up and down with her arm round me and her
head on my shoulder.

'That looks like a nice grassy bank,' she nodded.

'Yes, you're right.'

'Are you sure you won't have a tot?' Ruby enquired
when we were sitting down. I said not at the moment
and she took a long swig. 'I wonder,' Ruby remarked as
she replaced the stopper, 'how my hubby's getting on?
Know what I mean?'

'Oh ah.' I tried local vagueness.

'Probably frighten her to death,' Ruby speculated.

This made me laugh because, from what I had heard,
Miss Nook was quite a girl.

'That's better,' said Ruby. 'Hearing you laugh. You're
relaxing at last. I won't eat you. Just a bit of fun. Mustn't
miss opportunities, must we? Know what I mean?'

I did only too well. Ruby's proximity and availability,
the dark wood and the moonlight, made a heady
combination. We sat close together for a while and I
reminded her we must keep a lookout.

'Suppose so.' Ruby produced the hip flask and helped
herself to more brandy. 'Good stuff this. Keeps the old
cockles warm. Have some.'

'Not yet . . . '

'I'll have yours then.' Her voice was slurred. 'What's the time?'

'Twenty to twelve.'

'Only that?'

''Fraid so.'

'What are we going to do for the rest of the night?' Ruby snuggled up while continuing to swig the brandy. All too soon her voice was out of control and she began a rambling though revealing conversation. 'What do we – hubby and I – do all day? He looks into mouths. I look into the same mouths.'

'I'm not quite with you, Ruby.'

'Hubby. Dentist. I'm his hygienist. Think about it. About spending all your days scraping other people's teeth. Yuck! No wonder I want some light relief.'

Ruby turned to me then suddenly went rigid. I drew my head back to look at her face and saw eyes bulging out of sockets. Following her gaze, my eyes focused on the Monster.

It was less than thirty feet away and well over ten feet tall. The thing, with its huge bat-like head, moved past us towards the centre of the wood. As it began to disappear in the gloom I freed myself from Ruby and put the police whistle to my lips .

'No,' she whispered fearfully. 'It'll come here.'

'I must warn Stan and the others.'

Ruby fell back and curled herself up tightly as I blew the whistle and waved my torch. In the ensuing excitement I forgot about Ruby. There were other whistles blowing, lamps waving, people running and shouting.

The next few seconds were chaotic and I can only recall fragments of what happened. However my main impression was the Monster shrinking. As we converged on the hitherto terrifying creature, it became a wizened little man holding a net.

'What's the matter?' He blinked at the lights surrounding him. 'I'm a registered lepidopterist and I live near here. My name is Moriarty. Professor Moriarty.'

'A lepiwhat?' asked Stan Oakshott.

'Moth collector,' said Dr Prosser.

'It's the season,' his wife primly added.

While they were talking, I noted everyone was there apart from Ruby, her dentist husband and Miss Nook.

'Do you realise, Sir,' Stan addressed the Professor 'you have been frightening people up here? Prowling the wood. Waving your net. In the middle of the night.'

'What people?' Moriarty wanted to know. 'I've seen no one, but then I am very short-sighted. I simply hold my net aloft and the beautiful creatures fly into it. My home is nearby. Let us go there and sort this out in a civilised manner.'

'A good idea, Sir.' Stan moved off with the Professor, accompanied by the Prossers.

'This is a turn-up for the books,' Janis said to me.

'Where is Ruby?' asked Jackie.

'Back there,' I said vaguely, not quite sure where 'back' was. Fortunately Tiny was better orientated and, following the first group, we came upon Ruby still curled up fast asleep.

'What have you done to her?' Janis wanted to know.

'Nothing.'

'Perhaps that's the trouble,' Jackie said and they went into peals of laughter.

'Can't leave her here,' Tiny pulled Ruby to her feet. 'She reeks of brandy. And here's my best hip flask.'

Although Tiny had pulled Ruby to her feet with remarkable ease, it was not so simple keeping her there. Suspended between Tiny and me, she would suddenly sag. At the same time Ruby sang and talked to herself about for ever scraping teeth.

'What's she on about?' Janis asked me.

'Oh, something to do with her work.'

'More like something to do with her husband,' Jackie said, and the two sisters were back at their laughing.

'And Evadne?'

'Erotic Evadne.'

By then we had left the wood and were on the footpath leading to Upper Severnham Lane. Professor Moriarty, Stan Oakshott and the Prossers were about a hundred yards ahead, making their way to No 9 – the second house from this end.

'Plaque,' Ruby muttered. 'How I hate plaque.'

'Evadne Nook,' Janis giggled. 'To think we entrust our infants to her.'

'Someone's husband,' Jackie glanced at Ruby, 'won't be doing any more fillings tomorrow.'

'Give over,' growled Tiny. We continued having trouble with Ruby and were relieved to reach No 9. Getting her up the garden path, which had a series of shallow steps, took some time. The front door was open. As we reached it, a tall old lady came down the stairs. She was wearing fluffy slippers, frilly housecoat and a mop cap.

'Good evening,' the old lady greeted us. 'Are you with Ulysses?'

The unexpected name, coming on top of everything else, left me bemused. Janis and Jackie launched into more giggles, so it was fortunate Tiny kept his head.

'Yes Ma'am. Your husband invited us back here. My name's Palmer. From the farm below you.'

'Oh, the gorgeous Jersey herd! I'm Phoebe Moriarty. Do come in.'

Dame Phoebe did not appear to notice Ruby still suspended between us and Tiny had to explain about her as well.

'We had a . . . party. Ruby here is a little worse for wear.'

'Perhaps she would like to sleep it off,' said the Professor's wife, opening a side door. She spoke as if our arrival after midnight with a drunken woman was commonplace. We eased Ruby into a study and onto a leather sofa. There were moths everywhere – framed on the walls, contained in racks and being worked on at the desk. Phoebe waved her hand in their general direction.

'Ulysses is terribly keen.'

'Must be,' said Tiny, who at least was making an effort. I did not know what to say and the sisters continued giggling in the doorway.

'Leave her be,' Dame Phoebe said of Ruby, 'while we go in and join the others. What fun! A late night party.'

The room into which Phoebe showed us was a large one, made larger still by an extension at the back. Within the extension, draped round with blue velvet curtains like a concert platform, stood a grand piano and a cello, the latter held up by a wire stand. Sheets of music were strewn on nearby tables and chairs.

In the front part of the room, the Prossers and Oakshott were drinking sherry with Professor Moriarty. We were offered the same by Dame Phoebe who, like her husband, did not seem in the least worried she was wearing night apparel. They and the Prossers kept the conversation going until, during a lull, Stan demonstrated his powers of observation and deduction. Nodding at the piano and cello, he remarked to the Moriartys,

'You play then?'

'I should hope so,' Dame Phoebe assured him. 'Otherwise Cheltenham Boys College, not to forget the Ladies Coll, are paying us money under false pretences. Shall we play them something, Ulysses?'

'Would it appeal to our guests?'

The Prossers enthused and the rest of the guests nodded.

'The Schumann "Adagio", I think,' said Phoebe, sitting down behind the cello. She parted her housecoat, pulled up the night dress and positioned the instrument between bare legs. 'This is in A Flat Major. It represents Schumann's unmistakable blend of eloquent melancholy and spontaneous musical creativity. Come on, Ulysses. Let's have you.'

Despite the piece being a quiet one, the grand piano and cello made an astonishing amount of noise in the room. I was sitting on a sofa between Janis and Jackie. Each of us nursed a sherry and wore an interested expression.

However, as the 'Adagio' unwound, I began to wonder at the whole situation. We had set out to find the Severnham Monster and ended up listening to Schumann. I gazed fascinated at the Moriartys, both wearing little round spectacles as they peered at the music. While his feet fluttered on the piano pedals, her fluffy slippers also beat out the time.

Then I became aware of the sofa vibrating. It was caused by the sisters shaking with silent laughter. They were sitting close to me and first Jackie, then Janis, nudged me. The sofa shook all the more.

White Vans

'Have you noticed,' Edward Spinks asked me, 'the recent proliferation of white vans?'

We were standing at the entrance to his store. I looked up and down Severnham's short High Street and counted seven white vans.

'You will note,' Edward went on, 'how two of the vans – the one at the council offices and the other by the library – have names on the sides, while the further five are unmarked.'

'Is that significant?'

'I have a theory about white vans,' said Edward, 'and it is linked to the present state of the economy. The marked vans are run by people going about their legitimate business. They fill in tax forms, pay VAT and generally abide by the law.'

'And the others?'

'They tend to be cash only merchants. Mind you, I have quite a lot of sympathy for them. They are survivors bobbing about in the rough seas of recession. They have wives and families dependant on what they can win. Day by day.'

'You surprise me, Edward. Talking like that.'

'As a country, I'm afraid, we are over-regulated. There are far too many civil servants, council officers and the like skimming the cream off the milk. They make the rules to suit themselves. Impose restrictions to keep the rest of us in our places. You've seen it in Severnham which is our once Great Britain in miniature. Inevitably such a policy leads to white vans.'

This was a line of thought I had not previously followed. I was thinking about Edward's theory while walking from his store to my cottage. Thus seeing a white van parked in the garage drive came as a bit of a shock. A young man wearing a dark blue storm coat was leaning against the van. He stood up on my approach.

'Good morning, Sir.'

'Morning,' I said neutrally.

'I happened to be passing, Sir,' the young man explained, 'and noticed both your chimneys need re-pointing.'

'Do they?' I played for time.

'Oh yes, Sir. The main one urgently. It wouldn't stand another winter.'

'You think not?'

'Definitely not, Sir. A hard frost followed by a stiff blow and those top bricks would come tumbling down on to the roof. Then there'd be broken roof tiles and other structural damage to put right. Better to be safe than sorry, Sir.'

'Are you in this line of business, Mr . . . ?'

'Ted, Sir. Tell you what, I'd do your two chimneys for a hundred quid. By the weekend. And I'd make a good job of them. You could come up and see for yourself before paying me.'

I thought about it then said,

'I'd like to think about it.'

'Tell you what, Sir. I'll come down to eighty.'

'Mm.'

'Sixty.'

It was a sorry situation yet I had to smile.

'You'll be doing it for nothing next. Are you from around here and how long have you been repointing chimneys?'

'I live at Twiggleswood, Sir. I was formerly in the aircraft industry. Served a full technical apprenticeship. Was a toolmaker by trade. That was until they made me redundant. I used the money to buy this van. Since then I have been working on chimneys and other roof jobs as I don't mind heights. Sixty quid, Sir. Including all the necessary materials.

'You're talking cash, aren't you?'

'I'll do a good job.'

'I'm sure, Ted . . . if you were a toolmaker in the aircraft industry.'

'Easily prove that.' The young man produced a photo-copy of his trade certificate. It confirmed he had been a Grade I Toolmaker. Ted told me, 'With overtime and bonuses, I used to earn over £20,000 a year. Regular.'

'And now?'

'Still under six, Sir. But then I've only been on the chimneys the last ten months.'

'All right, Ted. If you're happy with sixty cash. When can you start?'

'This afternoon.' He glanced at a doubtful sky. 'Weather permitting.'

Such was the beginning of my introduction to the world of white vans. A week or so later, I was telling Polly at The Restoration what an excellent job Ted had done.

'Not only did he repoint the two chimneys, he also found and put right some defective guttering.'

'How much did it cost you in the end?'

'Close on a hundred quid.'

'Yes,' she nodded. 'White vanners always find more.'

I did not mind Polly putting me right because I admired her approach to life. Despite three disastrous marriages, she kept smiling. Polly had accepted a small cherry brandy and she listened with interest to my tale about Ted. Like most folk in Gloucestershire, Polly knew more that she made out. Unlike them however, she did release some of her inside information. Polly told me,

'Ted's a nice boy. He and his wife have three kids under the age of five. So it can't be easy for them. They took on far too much hire purchase apart from their mortgage. I warned them at the start.' She sipped her cherry brandy. 'It's time our chimneys here had some attention. I'll talk to Ronnie. When I manage to see him.'

Ronnie Twist managed The Restoration Inn owned by much grander and richer branches of the Twist family. He and his wife Hazel spent most of their days – and particularly nights commencing, consummating and concluding love affairs. It meant Polly ran the place.

111

However all monies needed had to come from the Twists through Ronnie. He was a generous man in other ways, but obtaining Twist cash was never easy.

Nevertheless Polly succeeded in having the inn chimneys repaired. For the next few weeks, Ted was up there with his scaffolding, trowel and cement. He would greet me with a cheery wave and I was glad for him.

The bizarre story which is about to unfold concerns Ted and the residents of Restoration Road. At one time it had been a no-through road and called Restoration Close. That was before Chief Councillor Conrad Twist wanted a more convenient run from his house on Severnham Hill to the council office.

Polly's neighbours include Dr and Mrs Prosser, our local dentist and his wife Ruby, also a retired wing commander. The Wing Co.'s house is opposite that of Polly and, to the right of him, lived a headmaster. In due course the headmaster moved to a bigger school and his house came on the market. Naturally the nosy people of Restoration Road – as indeed the rest of the village – wondered who would buy the property.

In order to tell what happened, it is necessary to say a little more about the road and its houses.

The houses on both sides of Restoration Road are large, stone-built, double-fronted and have semi-circular drives. The drives enter one gate and leave through the other. To the left of each property, an extension drive runs past its side door, leading into the kitchen area, and continues to a garage well set-back. The layout thus places the garages by the garden walls of their left-hand neighbours. In the case of the headmaster's garage, it is adjacent to the wing commander's back garden.

I mention all this because what subsequently transpired with the newcomer to Restoration Road will be all the more understandable.

One evening I decided to look in at The Restoration Inn. The lounge bar was fairly empty. The Prossers, the dentist and Ruby were sitting at a far table. Ruby gave me a merry wave which I acknowledged before turning to see who was at the bar. Ronnie was there as usual chatting up a sales girl. I recall him once telling me he was attracted to professional women. At the other end Hazel sat with her current choice, a well known hunk from Gloucester City's team.

In the centre of the bar Ted, without his overalls, was drinking and talking to Polly.

'What'll you have?' he greeted me.

I attempted to buy the drinks, but Ted would have none of it. He flipped a tenner from a roll of notes.

'You're in funds,' I remarked.

'Just been paid.' Ted lowered his voice. 'The Twists stumped up at last. This lot,' he returned the roll of notes to an inner pocket, 'will be in the bank tomorrow. But first, I owe you both drinks of thanks.'

'Tell him,' said Polly, 'about the person who has moved in opposite my place.'

'Oh ah,' Ted grinned. 'Monsieur Duval. Yes, a Froggy. Funny little fellow he is.'

'Little men can be very sexy,' Polly informed us.

'Not more than five foot,' Ted went on. Well dressed mind. Formal like. Black blazer and grey flannels. Dark faced chap with a moustache and one of them goat beards.'

'Goatee.'

'That's right. Speaks English with a heavy accent.'

'Lovely,' sighed Polly. 'Remember Charles Boyer?'

113

'Precise he was as well,' Ted continued. 'Knew exactly what he wanted with altering the garage.'

'What did he want?'

'The height of the doorway raised by forty centimetres. It's high already, but he was adamant. We went to the council offices together. Saw Arthur Tremblett. They wished to retain the lines of the road, but I put forward a scheme which was acceptable.'

'But why is he raising the lintel by forty centimetres?'

'Well you see, Monsieur Duval has a tall white van.'

It is peculiar how a particular fact remains in the mind. Every time there was a white van I thought of Monsieur Duval, even though as yet I had neither seen him nor his vehicle. In fact I did not see anything concerning Polly's neighbour for several days because, according to accounts, he went out during the late afternoon and returned in the early hours of the morning.

Yes, the people who had seen him said he had a tall rather narrow van. Of French make they thought. It was driven by a man wearing a white coat, black beret and dark glasses.

Then one Saturday evening, I was passing The Restoration, with no intention of going inside, when I noticed Polly by the front entrance. There was, I knew, a rugby club party going on which meant a lot of noise. Polly said,

'I came out for a breather.'

'Noisy,' I said.

'Very much so,' she agreed. 'I'm glad to see you. I wanted to talk to you about my new neighbour, Monsieur Duval.'

'How are things there?'

'That's what I'd like to discuss. Look, would you

come round and have coffee with me tomorrow morning? About eleven.'

'Certainly. Love to.'

'Correction. At a quarter to . . . no, twenty to if you can.'

'Of course I can. Is the alteration significant?'

'The Wing Co's coming at eleven. I'd like to brief you first.'

I arrived at Polly's shortly after ten-thirty. She was pleased by my being early and we went to a window seat in the lounge. From there we could see when the wing commander put in an appearance. It also gave us a good view of Duval's house.

'There's something not quite right about him,' said Polly, 'and it worries me. He arrived ten days ago and, when he sees one of us outside, introduces himself. He saw me in the front garden and came across to take my hand and kiss the back of it. Very flattering, but then he held on to my hand and looked hard at me. He has deep dark liquid eyes which seem to go right through a person. The neighbours say the same.

'Well that was fair enough. It's his other activities which worry me. I have time off in the afternoons – between two and six. That is also the time when Duval departs in his tall white van. He backs it out of that garage and turns into the space behind the house. Before going into the space he closes and locks the garage so the van blocks any view into it. Once at the rear of the house, he is again hidden.

'He then takes up to half an hour loading the van. It is done quietly but methodically. At last, wearing a white dust coat, black beret and dark glasses, he leaves the premises. Duval stops to lock the front gates and I think he has some sort of security system because lights go on and off during the night. He returns, sometimes at two or three in the morning – quietly – but I've not been sleeping too well waiting for him.'

'I'm sure there's nothing to worry about, Polly. The man's probably going about his lawful business.'

'There's more,' she said. 'I have seen other people. A tall girl. To tell the truth, I saw her arrive. It was after three in the morning. When I couldn't sleep. As I heard the van I got up and looked across. I thought there was someone in the front passenger seat. Duval unlocked the gate and there she was. I saw her get out by the garage. The tall girl. Duval opened the kitchen door and she disappeared into the house.'

'Men have been known to bring girls home . . . ' I began.

'I never saw her again, but there was another. Again tall but very young. Just a kid I would think. She stood staring out of that top left-hand bedroom window. One afternoon. As the van was leaving. It was weird. I nearly went across, but of course I couldn't.'

'Not really,' I agreed. 'Perhaps Duval has a family?'

'Mm.' Polly sounded doubtful. 'I wanted to tell you before the wing commander arrives. After all he lives next door and I have seen him talking to Duval. He might enlighten us.'

'The Wing Co. is taciturn and phlegmatic,' I warned her. 'Doesn't say much.'

'I thought,' Polly gave her wonderful smile, 'we could egg him on a bit. Without letting on, you understand. It'd be easier with the two of us. But don't tell him you know what I told you, will you?'

The wing commander duly arrived and we had coffee

and talked for over an hour. His contributions on the subject of Monsieur Duval amounted to the following paragraph.

'Interesting chap. Some sort of technician. Jolly clever with his hands. Mended my outside light. Never worked in years. Also the fencing between my garden and his garage. Mine really but he turned up with new panels. Did the job in an afternoon. Wouldn't take a penny. What about tall girls? Ah yes. Couple of crackers.'

After the wing commander had left, I said to Polly,

'He's not worried, so you shouldn't get wound up.'

'I've been around. Duval makes me uneasy.' She bit her lip.

We left it at that. More, though not much more, came out in the weeks following. Our vicar, Andrew Mead, called on Duval and learned the newcomer was RC. Edward Spinks began delivering groceries to the house. One girl sauntered through Severnham on a Saturday morning, causing heads to turn. That was before she disappeared to be replaced by an even taller girl. Then she too vanished and a well dressed woman put in an appearance. For a time.

'Interesting chap,' said Edward exactly as the Wing Co. had done. 'The tailgate of my estate was not working properly. He spotted it, went in for a screwdriver and made an adjustment. Right away.'

'Strange,' I said.

'They're different I suppose. His first name's Maurice by the way. One of the girls called to him from an inside room. I've never been further than the kitchen door myself.'

Edward was telling me this in his store. When he had finished, Elizabeth added,

'I know a little about France. My mother was half French. The Duvals are Parisians. The patois . . . '

'But what are they doing here?'

'We're in the European Union now,' she reminded me. 'They have every right to come and work here.'

Two small events took place during the next fortnight. They were minor ones not affecting the main issue but, as they both involved white vans, I shall mention them.

With the first, Maurice Duval asked the wing commanded if he knew of a local toolmaker who could set up some small precision machinery. The Wing Co. told him that Ted, who had worked on the garage, was formerly a toolmaker. Polly then saw Ted's white van parked opposite and later asked him what was going on.

'It seems,' she told us, 'Duval is setting up a little workshop round the back of his place. Nothing big, though Ted did enquire if he had official approval and was shown one from the council. Funny, don't you think?'

'Strange,' I said once more.

The next white van event in Restoration Road took place shortly afterwards. I am mentioning the incident because it is typical of our times. Polly saw a small white van on the road outside the Duval's house. As she watched two boys came running out, leapt into the van and tore away through the village.

Polly was still taking this in when Stan Oakshott came up the road on his bicycle. He only lived round the corner and, as we later learned, the Duval security system was connected to the police house.

'Did you see anything?' Stan asked and Polly told him

what she had witnessed. 'Oh ah,' he nodded matter-of-factly, 'they will be the Myers boys.'

'Then you can go and arrest them.'

'Not as easy as that,' Stan told her.

The attempted break-in and Stan's reply became a talking point at The Restoration Inn. We heard PC Oakshott of the Yard had put in a report. But why, we demanded, have they not been arrested? At last, Stan explained.

'The Myers are a Gloucester family headed by Ma Myers. Every member is a villain, well known to the police. The two boys Polly saw are untouchable. They're under age, you see. So the Myers send them out on recce patrols. Oh ah. Greater brains than mine ensure their protection from the law.'

At least the incident helped Ted in his white van. He became busy installing other security systems.

Polly's reaction to the two minor events differed from the rest of us. She brooded on them and one evening asked me,

'Why does Duval have a fitted workshop in his house? Why is his security system connected to the police station?'

'Why don't you ask him?'

'I couldn't. He's not that sort of man.'

'What sort do you think he is then? You women generally have it all worked out. In a split second.' When Polly did not respond, I added, 'Why not ask Stan?'

'I have,' said Polly, 'and was told Monsieur Duval keeps strictly within the law.'

I have previously mentioned how Duval would load up his tall white van and leave during the late afternoon to wherever he was going. This period coincided with

Polly's off-duty period from The Restoration. Normally she would either relax at home or do household tasks. But Polly had become so intrigued by Duval she decided on another course of action.

Polly had a tiny car, the smallest Fiat, which she kept in her garage because there was little need for it. However one afternoon she ran up the car and parked it outside on the road. When Duval went through his routine and set off in the van, Polly jumped into her car and followed him.

'He turned left at the High Street,' she told me, 'in the direction of Twiggleswood. Round the bend he went. Past the church and your place.'

'Did he see you?'

'Oh no! I kept well back. It was easy following his tall van. Anyway, as I was saying, he went past your cottage and up the lane to the main road. Duval turned left there and I kept further back because it is more open. We went on and on until, to my horror, he took a slip road on to the motorway. Before I realised it, I was also on the motorway. Travelling towards the Midlands.'

'In your little Fiat.'

'Midge I call her,' said Polly. 'She was as shocked as I was. Especially when Duval put his foot down. He began to pull away and poor Midge was protesting. In the end I turned off at Worcester and came back here. Had to, for I was due to start work at six.'

'So Duval goes up to the Midlands,' I said. 'At least you learned that.'

'Which isn't a lot,' Polly pointed out.

She was obviously caught up in the mystery and I tried telling her not to rush it.

'For goodness sake, Polly,' I said. 'It'll all come out in

due course. He seems a capable and friendly sort of man.'

'It's those girls who worry me,' Polly said. 'They come and then they disappear. I know what I am going to say sounds silly, but . . . ' she bit her lip before asking, 'what if we have a serial killer in our midst?'

The next incident concerning Monsieur Duval came all too swiftly. When Polly rang me, not long after eleven one night, she sounded half hysterical.

'I've done something very silly,' she babbled, 'and now I'm terrified.'

'What is it, Polly?'

'Could you come here? I don't know what to think.'

'I'm on my way,' I said. Actually I had been on my way to bed. Slipping on a coat and snatching up a torch, I hurried from the cottage to Restoration Road. There I found Polly with a large brandy.

'The wing commander is away,' she explained. 'He asked me to keep an eye on his place. I have the keys and I've been going over there during the day. But this evening I had my silly idea. There's a high window on the side of Duval's garage accessible from the Wing Co.'s garden. Using a ladder . . . Well, Duval was out and the wing commander has a light ladder . . . '

'You didn't?'

'I did.' Polly took a generous gulp of brandy. 'I leant the ladder next to Duval's garage window, climbed up with a torch and shone it inside. The first objects I saw, hanging on the opposite wall, were manacles. Then I directed the beam downwards and there . . . there was an open coffin. But worse still, I looked towards the back of the garage and what do you think I saw? A French guillotine!'

121

After I had digested what Polly told me, I suggested she must inform Stan Oakshott. Polly was reluctant at first, but eventually allowed me to ring Stan. Oakshott of the Yard is one of those people who can appear day or night, fully clothed and perfectly calm. He listened to Polly's story before remarking mysteriously,

'Now I suppose it'll have to come out.'

'What will?' I asked him.

'Best I get his permission.' Stan did not appear to hear.

'You won't let on about me, will you?' Polly asked him with instant feminine practicability.

Stan shook his head then suddenly looked at her.

'Did you put away the ladder?'

'No. I forgot. The shock . . . '

'Oh dear, oh dear,' said our village policeman. 'Leaving evidence lying about.'

I tried to get more out of Stan as we were removing and stowing away the Wing Co.'s ladder, but he did not elucidate.

'Best to clear it with Duval first,' was all I learned.

A few days went by with no more news. Duval continued on his journeys. Polly was on tenterhooks. Our curiosity grew. The next stage was a surprising one. Posters appeared round the village – on the council office notice board, outside the library and health centre, at the church hall. They announced a special performance by Maurice Duval. Illusionist.

The performance – price £2 adults and £1 children, all seats – would be in aid of the church roof fund. It transpired that Maurice Duval and his family were famous throughout France for a series of amazing illusions, devised and produced solely by himself. With the lowering of European barriers, the Duvals had decided to perform in British theatres and clubs. They were enjoying great success around the Midlands, after which they would tour the West Country and Wales.

The Duval family came to help Maurice prepare the church hall. No one else was allowed to be there, not even Andrew Mead, who was doing a vintage car refit. Monsieur Duval showed polite interest in the motor, as it was a pre-World War II Renault, but the car and tools had to be removed elsewhere.

As news of the forthcoming entertainment became more widespread – with the local rag featuring The Astounding Duval – our chief councillor had to get in on the act. The question of a performing licence raised its head, but was settled by Conrad Twist and his party acquiring the whole of the first row. The Meads, Polly and I queued early and managed to make the fifth. The rest of the hall was packed.

Eventually the curtains parted and Monsieur Duval in full evening attire appeared to greet us. He was accompanied by several members of his family, the tall girls in black tights with fish net stockings and high heeled shoes. Madame Duval – for it was she – wore an evening gown of black velvet.

It is impossible to describe that magical evening. So many astonishing feats were done before our eyes. Duval began by saying how those occupying the front row of such a show had to pay the price. His two tall daughters then enticed Councillor Conrad Twist on to the stage.

'You will note,' said the illusionist, 'how I am standing well away from this distinguished gentleman in order not to influence the trick he is about to perform.'

Under Duval's directions, Twist took off his wrist

watch, put it in a black velvet bag, placed the bag on a wood block and hit it several times with a mallet. Then the bag, block and mallet were whirled away by the assistants and Duval told Twist to take the original watch out of an inside pocket.

After that opening, one amazing illusion followed another. Monsieur Duval was padlocked in heavy manacles, the girls held up a black cloth, dropped it and he was free. Madame Duval lay in the wooden box and its lid was nailed over her. Only her head showed at one end and her feet at the other.

Monsieur Duval next proceeded to saw the box in half. He draped two cloths over the cut ends – 'so as not to disturb the younger members of the audience' – before pulling the boxes apart on two trolleys. The halved Madame Duval was separated and rolled around the stage. All the while she smiled benignly, nodding her head and waggling her feet.

The grand finale was the guillotine. A red, white and blue drape at the back of the stage was dropped to reveal the grim machine. After trundling the guillotine to front stage, Duval demonstrated its ability to cut cabbages clean in half. After that he said his guillotine was a magic one which would not chop off anyone's head. Who would like to try it out? No one stirred. Duval pleaded with the audience then produced a wad of notes which he opened like a fan.

'Here is my sponsorship towards your church roof fund. It will go to the person who is brave enough to lie under the guillotine.'

'I'll do it for the church roof fund.' Dottie rose from beside me and made her way to the stage.

While she lay with her neck in the clamp, Monsieur

Duval led a sponsorship auction which raised several hundred more pounds. Eventually, with us all holding our breaths, he pulled the lever. The blade fell, passing through the wooden clamp and presumably Dottie's neck. Much later she told us how.

'The illusion was fixed up between Duval and myself. The blade is of silvered rubber, the weight balsa wood. There are two blades. The first falls into the clamp above the neck and displaces the second below the neck.'

'But the cabbages,' I said. 'They were cut clean in half.'

'Beforehand,' said Dottie, 'then stuck back. Using the lever knocked off the front half. As for Twist's watch trick, it's so simple I don't know how you were all taken in.'

Dangerous Liaison

Severnham District lies within a great loop of the river. A main road runs across the top as if it does not want to know us. Our most prominent feature is Severnham Hill which results in the rest being made up of varying slopes. These are steep by the hill, less so across farmlands and built on areas, then flat and low beside the stream.

Visitors to Severnham Village often remark how, after the short High Street, the surroundings get a bit tacky, what with the bungalows and smallholdings of the Flukes. After that, down to the river, the countryside becomes strangely deserted.

'Why,' ask people on summer day visits, 'is no one living near to or even beside such a lovely river?'

A short answer is the Severn is deceptive. It floods at least once yearly and about every quarter of a century covers the lower part of our loop. Young yuppie couples living in the Meadowsweet Estate at Lower Severnham are due for a bad shock sometime in their lives. Meanwhile the Twists who built those houses took the money and moved to higher ground.

There is another interesting factor connected with the lower part of the Severnham Loop. In the past, certain people used to come and spend their summers near its end. Knowing country ways, they did so after the threat of winter flooding had passed. These people were the genuine gipsies.

During recent times, the gipsies have been – how shall I put it – discouraged. The powers-that-be prefer sitting ducks to mobile ones. Paperwork and persuasion was applied with the consequence that the number of gipsy families diminished then disappeared. However one morning my nearest neighbour, Samuel Hopskip and a man of few words, remarked over the garden hedge,

'Them travellers are back.'

'Oh ah.' I did not try to learn more. Details would emerge later, either from him or someone else.

The next I heard was when PC Stan Oakshott came round 'to have a word.'

'It's the Moores,' he said.

'Who are the Moores?'

'The gipsy family what's moved into Loop End.'

'Oh. Will it affect me?'

'The men'll come touting for work and their women trying to sell things. Be polite to the men. Don't touch the women.'

I thanked Stan for his well-meant advice. An hour later a swarthy individual came to my front gate.

'Morning Sir. Any jobs you'd like done?'

'What sort can you do?' I asked.

'Garden,' he replied. 'Your hedges need trimming. If you've got shears or a hook, I'll do them for . . . ' he paused, ' . . . for ten quid.' It took him exactly two hours.

My next gipsy sighting was mid-week. I had gone for some groceries after which Edward Spinks and I were chatting by the door. The High Street was quite busy and this made it all the more strange when everyone stopped to stare. Walking our way along the street came a gipsy girl.

The girl was as slim as a wand and swayed accordingly. Raven black hair fell to her waist. Coal black eyes looked disdainfully at all around her. She was wearing a white blouse and a colourful embroidered skirt. Her brown legs were bare apart from slip-on sandals.

'They have three motorised caravans at Loop End,' Edward told me. 'Each with a trailer. There are about fifteen to twenty of them.'

'And who's this one?' I asked.

'Don't know,' he replied. 'Did you see that nature film last night? The one where the female cheetah walks surveying the herd of deer. Well, this girl looks the same.'

The gipsy went past us and we watched her go into The Restoration. For the purpose of continuity, I will tell what Polly told me about her arrival there. Polly was polishing glasses in the bar when the girl entered.

'My brother said there is a job going here.'

'Yes,' Polly confirmed. 'What can you do?'

'Work,' the girl replied.

The job was that of kitchen maid, the lowest in the place, but the girl accepted it and the money without comment.

Her name was Hannah Moore. She worked hard and did not talk much. The other members of staff tried pulling her leg, but there is no satisfaction when the recipient does not respond. Soon they left Hannah alone and began to like her.

I have not mentioned the rest of the staff before and will do so now because this provides a background. There were nine headed by Polly. After her came the chief cook in the form of Mrs Molloy, a large lady more at home with bread-and-butter puddings than charlotte russe. She was assisted by Robin Pender, a limp-wristed trainee chef who spoke of 'my mousses' and 'my soufflés' as if they were parts of his anatomy. Then there was Mr Molloy the cleaner of shoes and cars, also the driver of the courtesy bus. The Molloy's niece Bridget saw to the reception of guests. She was polite but so chilly with it, the others called her Frigid Bridget. Finally there were two chambermaids and two waitresses – four pert streetwise Flukes.

When Hannah Moore started at The Restoration Inn, Ronnie and Hazel Twist were both absent. He had gone on a study tour of European hotels organised by the top sales lady at some food chain. Hazel had accompanied a friend to the Algarve. The first to return was Hazel and Polly told her about their new member of staff.

'I understand she'll only be here for the summer then they move on.'

'That's fine,' Hazel said. 'Summer's our busiest time.'

Two days later Hazel Twist was in the kitchen and

noticed Hannah Moore working quietly there. Hazel went over to her and said,

'I believe you're a genuine gipsy?'

'Yes.'

'Can you tell fortunes?'

'Yes.'

'Would you do mine?'

'It's a pound for the hand,' Hannah replied, 'and five if I use the crystal ball.'

Hazel laughed before saying,

'You've got yourself a crystal ball customer. Bring it to work and tell mine.'

Next morning Hazel and Polly were in the office behind the reception desk when they heard Bridget coldly arguing with someone. Hazel went out to learn what was happening and saw Hannah standing there with her crystal ball. The gipsy girl was invited into the office and Polly asked to stay.

'You can be a witness,' Hazel laughed. 'Tell me Hannah, do you really see my future swirling round in the crystal?'

'No,' Hannah answered.

'Then what do you see in there?'

'Nothing.'

'Nothing?'

'It is used to help clear my mind.'

Hazel and Polly glanced at each other while Hannah gazed into the crystal. At least a minute went by before Hannah spoke without looking at Hazel. According to Polly, the girl said,

'You are going to have a long and serious illness, which you will enjoy.'

'Enjoy?' Hazel queried. 'An illness?'

'After your illness, you will go on a long journey.'

'They always say a long journey,' Hazel remarked to Polly.

'To the end of the world,' Hannah insisted. 'Your life will change completely. Completely,' she repeated.

'What about romance?' Hazel wanted to know and was told,

'There is going to be a different kind of love. I cannot understand it.' Hannah frowned at the crystal. 'Different. That is all I can tell you.'

In order to maintain the story sequence, it is necessary to follow this thread for a while. Others will arise in due course to form a whole fabric.

Polly told me how Hazel had complained of a cold spoiling the holiday even in sunny Algarve. A month after Hazel came back to Severnham the cold was still with her. She then made an appointment to see Doctor Prosser. He listened to her voice and chest before recommending X-rays. Hazel went privately and within an hour learned the result.

'I'm afraid,' said the doctor at the private clinic, 'you have TB.'

'Fortunately these days,' Dr Prosser told Hazel, 'we can beat TB with drugs. I have no doubt we shall do the same in your case. But it will mean taking you out of circulation.'

'What does it entail?'

'Bed rest during the treatment. For at least six to eight weeks.'

'Is that necessary, Doctor? I had a friend with the same complaint. She didn't have to rest at all. And she was cured in a month.'

'She was lucky. Probably a slight infection. Yours has taken hold. Quite serious . . . '

Hazel Twist was accordingly taken out of circulation. She went into a private nursing home and Polly visited her every other day. Their main topic of conversation was The Restoration Inn, but early on Hazel asked,

'Is that gipsy girl still with you?'

'Yes. Hannah is a good worker.'

'Funny how she predicted my illness.'

'Not funny for you, Hazel.'

'Not bad either. There's nothing to the treatment and I am responding well they tell me. The staff here are super . . . and I have learned a valuable lesson.'

'What lesson?'

'About boyfriends. Do you know Polly, not one has come to see me. It's as if I've got the plague.'

What of Ronnie Twist? Well, he completed his study tour of European hotels with the lady executive and returned to The Restoration Inn. After Hazel went into the nursing home, Ronnie did call when – as he put it – he could. He would bring far too many flowers, also make sure the nurses knew his wife was out of circulation. Polly told me such behaviour was more typical than most people realised.

However, within minutes of re-entering The Restoration, Ronnie discovered Hannah Moore. He was a man well endowed with female-seeking antennae.

'Who is this?' Ronnie enquired of Mrs Molloy as he looked across the kitchen at Hannah. 'New talent, I see.'

'Talent for hard work,' said the no-nonsense cook.

'And what is your name, my dear?' Ronnie turned to Hannah.

'Moore, Sir.'

'More, Sir.' Ronnie could not resist the double meaning. 'Surely you have a forename?'

'Hannah, Sir.'

'Hannah.' Ronnie savoured the name. 'My first Hannah.'

He went on to tell her how the welfare of the staff was always near to his heart. How his office door was ever open. How she should never hesitate to come and see him. Particularly as his wife was out of circulation.

'He's an old lecher,' the Fluke girls said to Hannah. 'We work in pairs round here. Especially upstairs.'

Such was the situation following Hazel's departure and Ronnie's return. A third influence was the Severnham District Council. Certain officials were not happy about the gipsies at Loop End. There could be the breaking of several by-laws. Take hygiene for example. Loop End had no toilets. Neither did it have running water – apart from the River Severn.

Because none of the officials fancied confronting the gipsies, the Severnham District Council referred the matter to the National Rivers Authority who passed it to the Department of the Environment who sent it back to the Severnham District Council.

The file, with each recipient calling for a further report, at last landed on the desk of Chief Councillor Conrad Twist. He went into his usual blow-up mode and summoned the long-suffering Arthur Tremblett.

'Tremblett, I see this file has been twice across your desk. When it started here and when it came back. You should have acted the first time. Your failure to act has made my council look foolish.'

'Er, what sort of action, Mr Twist?'

'There must be some legal application.'

'No one has quite established that, Mr Twist.'

'Well I have now.' Conrad Twist's pen with the broad nib descended on the uppermost document. He wrote, 'Pass to PC Oakshott for appropriate action. CT.'

Apart from being a cautious character, Stan Oakshott was an old hand at local politics. When Arthur Tremblett came to brief him, he immediately objected.

'Them gipsies haven't put a foot wrong, Arthur.'

'I wouldn't quite say that, Stan. Apart from them being there illegally . . . '

'How illegally?'

'We have many by-laws . . . '

'Come off it, Arthur. They're well out of our way. Living quietly. Doing odd jobs. Keeping down the rabbit population.'

'It's the principle, Stan. If we allow three vehicles this summer, there'll be thirty the next. Go and have a word with whoever is in charge. Ask them to leave quietly before we are obliged to obtain an official eviction order.'

'Why me, Arthur? Why not you?'

'Because Mr Twist has written your name, Stan.'

It was an unwinnable argument. Oakshott of the Yard knew that though he did not like it. Nevertheless he got on his bike and cycled slowly out to Loop End.

There the three motorised caravans with their big trailers were parked as if to ward off an enemy attack. Gipsy men, women and children watched Stan prop his bike against a tree and take off his clips. He looked around him. The site was clean and tidy, better than many so-called civilised places Stan could name.

Grandpa Moore sat outside the biggest caravan. He got up and courteously said to Stan,

'Take a seat. You've cycled a long way.'

'Oh ah,' Stan agreed.

'Would you like a glass of lemonade, beer or dandelion wine?'

'Lemonade would do fine . . . knowing the strengths of your homemade beers and wines.'

The gipsy leader smiled and ordered lemonade which arrived well chilled.

'How do you get it so cold?' Stan enquired.

'We hang the bottles in the river,' he was informed.

'Very welcome. Cheers.'

'Cheers,' said Grandpa Moore and sat down beside him.

Eventually Stan got round to the reason for his visit. He said the officials were becoming difficult. Talking of court orders. Grandpa Moore said that was unreasonable. They had kept out of the way. There had been no stealing. No complaints. The site was as clean as the day they arrived.

Stan Oakshott agreed and sympathised. However, he said, the council was worried about more gipsies turning up next summer. The gipsy leader replied he could not speak for any others. His people had planned to stay until the autumn before moving to winter quarters in Cornwall. Stan thought this was reasonable and promised to report back to the council.

While speaking to Grandpa Moore, Stan Oakshott noticed something which interested him. At the other side of the circle four young gipsies had lowered the ramp of a trailer inside which were two magnificent motor bikes. Harley Davidsons, Stan thought. Before leaving the encampment he strolled over to look at them. They were indeed Harley Davidsons.

'I envy you,' he remarked to the men. They half smiled but were not over friendly. Stan had heard the gipsies used to come into Severnham on motor bikes – to buy what they wanted and to drop the girl off at The Restoration. It was a little fact to bear in mind.

The owners of the Harley Davidsons watched as Stan put on trouser clips, mounted his push bike and began the long haul from Loop End back to Severnham Village.

Edward Spinks told me later how PC Oakshott had reported to Arthur Tremblett who then had a word with Conrad Twist. At the time, our Chief Councillor was busy entertaining opposite numbers from other Gloucestershire councils and said to Arthur,

'Can't you see I'm busy?'

So Tremblett left it at that and the gipsy site won a temporary reprieve. Hannah Moore went on working at the inn. Ronnie Twist continued to pester Hannah whenever he saw her. Hazel Twist remained at the nursing home feeling better than she had done for years. Her skin glowed and she put on just enough weight to live with it.

'She looks so much better,' Polly told me after a visit to the nursing home and I remarked,

'It's strange how the gipsy girl knew.'

'Hazel did look unwell.'

'Even so . . . There was also the long journey.'

'I don't know about that one,' Polly laughed.

But she was not laughing on her return from the next visit to Hazel.

'Listen to this,' Polly said. 'There is a temporary doctor at the home who's befriended Hazel. Scottish. Clean cut. Far too young for her. Anyway, he goes overseas with medical teams. Most people in this country, he told Hazel, have no idea how the rest of the world lives. Or rather exists.'

'You're not going to tell me . . . ?'

'I am,' Polly insisted. 'Patagonia of all places. In ten weeks time. After she's finished treatment. The specialist is quite happy to let her go. Make a complete break, he says.'

'What'll happen here?'

'Who knows?'

What did happen was not very clever. Ronnie had become increasingly difficult in Hazel's absence. Her departure to the far end of the world made him insufferable. The Restoration Inn was running smoothly, largely due to Polly's work behind the scenes. Now Polly and the rest of the staff had to put up with Ronnie's 'improvements'.

Polly Clements is an easy-going person. She put up with Ronnie taking on Miranda, a glamorous though useless barmaid. She turned a blind eye to the succession of nubile catering students who kept appearing and disappearing. However Polly did warn Ronnie to keep his hands off Hannah Moore.

'She's quiet, honest and hard working. Let's not spoil it, shall we?'

'What do you mean, Polly?'

'You know very well what I mean. There's another aspect. I understand gipsies are very protective people. Harm one of them and the others will make you suffer for it.'

Ronnie dismissed the idea with a laugh and waited his chance. Since Hazel's departure with the medical team to South America, Polly had not been going to the nursing home every other afternoon. But she did have Mondays off and Ronnie Twist decided to strike then.

On the Monday morning in question, Ronnie came bustling into the kitchen and, ignoring Mrs Molloy, said to Hannah,

'Come on, Hannah. You're going to earn your keep. I've got to pick up some liqueurs from the wholesalers in Gloucester and need a hand.' He turned to Mrs Molloy. 'All right with you?'

'With respect Sir, that's not her job.'

'I say what is everyone's job round here,' Ronnie replied. 'Come on Hannah. I'm in a hurry. It'll give you a chance to see how my BMW can travel.'

No one discovered what happened in the next three hours. Therefore I must stick to the known facts. Fact 1. At 10.35 a.m. Ronnie left with Hannah. Fact 2. At 1.30 p.m. Ronnie returned without Hannah. Fact 3. Ronnie rushed upstairs holding a blood stained handkerchief to the side of his face.

Bridget Molloy in reception sent for Polly. Then Polly, trying to unravel the tangle, went up to what had been the Twists' suite. Ronnie however would not open the door. He shouted out to her instead.

'Hannah's not coming back! I've sent that gipsy bitch packing. Given her the sack.'

'You can't do that,' Polly told him.

'I've done it,' he told her. 'Go away.'

Polly walked slowly down the stairs because she was trying to think through the situation.

'Miranda,' she said to the new dumb barmaid, 'you'll have to cope while I go and see about Hannah.'

'Oh dear,' said Miranda. 'I get so muddled.'

I am telling this as Polly told me. She went to the

office and worked out what money was owing to Hannah. She then got in her little Fiat and set off for Loop End.

'I was worried as I drove there,' said Polly, 'and more worried when I arrived.'

'Why was that?'

'The gypsies had gone.'

According to Polly, the site was almost as if no one had ever been there. Not a tin, a bottle or a scrap of paper could be seen around the place. Earth had been thrown over ashes and raked across tyre marks.

'I sat in the car and cried,' said Polly. 'I found it incredibly sad.'

Unbeknown to us, the gipsies had been sent packing by Conrad Twist. A master of useless detail, our Chief Councillor kept a follow-up file. This ensured every action he initiated had to be completed and confirmed. Or else . . .

Arthur Tremblett and Stan Oakshott were summoned to stand on the Persian carpet in front of the Regency desk. Afterwards the council's solicitor produced an eviction notice which Stan then had to serve on Grandpa Moore.

Stan later related how he did notice Hannah was on the site when she should have been working in The Restoration. At the time he did not put much store on it. Neither did he understand when the gipsy chief re-marked, more in sorrow than anger, it was not right getting the girl to walk back from Gloucester.

'I didn't know what he was on about,' Stan told the Spinks and me. 'It's a good few miles. She looked angry and so did the four young men.'

'Who are they?' he had asked Grandpa Moore.

'Her brothers,' came the stern reply.

The situation at six that evening was as follows. Hannah had gone, the gipsies departed and Ronnie Twist was still upstairs in his suite. Polly and Stan were trying to work out what to do while I listened. Presently Edward Spinks joined me and he listened as well.

We were on our second round when Edward suddenly remarked,

'Polly, you did say Ronnie was upstairs with a scratched face?'

'Yes. He's keeping a low profile. Won't be showing himself for a day or two I reckon.'

'Well, his BMW is not outside.'

'It is.'

'It isn't.'

We duly trooped out and Edward was proved right.

'Now,' Stan sighed, 'I'll have to do something.' This concerned Oakshott whose pride and joy lay in never having to arrest anyone. He slowly finished his ale and left us.

Half an hour later, Stan returned for another ale.

'Panic over,' he reported. 'The gipsy convoy has been intercepted near Bristol. No sign of the BMW. No one knows anything.'

'Quite a coincidence,' Edward mused.

'Someone else must have nicked it,' Stan said. 'Holmes – the national police computer – has been informed. So we'll just have to wait and see.'

Oakshott of the Yard is usually right, but this time he was dead wrong. Again the facts. Fact 1. Ronnie had never left the suite. Fact 2. His BMW had disappeared. Fact 3. The Bristol police said the gipsies were now

140

camped for the night. The site had been thoroughly searched. There was no sign of the car.

What happened next has been told and retold by the locals. I shall start with what I witnessed. Back in my cottage as dusk fell, I was about to pull the curtains when I saw a fire on Severnham Hill. As I watched, the flames began to move. They ran from the top of the hill all the way down to one of Tiny Palmer's fields. On their downward path, the flames passed between two houses along Upper Severnham Lane.

The flaming BMW had in fact nearly rammed into the back of Conrad Twist's house. It missed by a whisker, but swept away a cold frame and garden shed. The torched car then shot across the lane, through a hedge and continued careering until it met a stone wall. The wall was hardly damaged. By then however, Ronnie's pride and joy had become a write-off.

Conrad Twist went berserk. Police cars, fire engines and the curious like myself went to investigate. I noticed Stan standing respectfully on one side as our chief councillor continued to harangue everyone within earshot.

'This has become serious,' I whispered to Stan.

'Not really,' he whispered back. 'No one saw or heard anything. No evidence, I'm afraid.'

Now that Conrad Twist was involved, he worried away at the problem. His high level contacts in the county were roused from their beds for further efforts. Police paid two more calls to the gipsy site – one that night and the other early in the morning. The Moore family could not understand. They had been twenty-five miles away when the incident took place.

Unable to pin anything on the gipsies, Conrad turned

his wrath on Ronnie. He swept into the hotel and demanded to see this lesser member of the Twist family. Ronnie duly arrived with patches of plaster across his face. The two Twists went into the office and were closeted there for well over an hour. Eventually Conrad swept out again leaving Ronnie a broken man. Hazel had left The Restoration Inn and now Ronnie went.

Polly and the rest of the staff wondered what would occur next. Management consultants, specializing in the hotel and catering trades, were called in. The consultants' findings, which first went to Conrad Twist, were not critical. In fact they recommended promoting Polly.

But Polly was not over keen and a part-time manager came to assist her. For some reason, a complete refurbishment was put in hand. It included an improved restaurant and extended car park. In the end, The Restoration Inn looked much the same as it had before, only a little brighter.

Readers may care to know what happened to Ronnie and Hazel after their departure from Severnham.

Ronnie simply sank out of sight. Someone said he had gone with Miranda to London. Another thought he had found work in a Birmingham betting shop. As for Hazel, she never came back to Severnham. I did see her once on television. There was a film about disaster workers somewhere in Africa. All of a sudden I spotted Hazel surrounded by native children.

The villagers often talked about the gipsy incident in the oblique way they have. I particularly recall a conversation on the subject with Oakshott of the Yard. He had stopped by on a hot summer afternoon when a can of chilled lager does not come amiss. Stan referred to how

the torched BMW had been pushed down behind
Conrad Twist's house.

'It must have been Hannah's brothers who did it,' he
mused. 'Yet they couldn't have been in two places at
once. Even with them Harley Davidsons. Could they?'

'You tell me, Stan.' He did not, so I went on, 'Lucky
the car missed. Could have done a lot of damage if it had
crashed into the back of Conrad's house.'

'Oh ah,' Stan agreed. 'Inconvenienced him like.'

'Romeo and Juliet'

Misses Menage and Nook teach at Severnham Village
School. They are a couple of local characters and long
may they remain so. Nora Menage appears more formidable with her thick black eyebrows and moustache.
The children pretend to go in fear of her, but they know
she is caring and kind. In later years they extol her
virtues. As for Evadne Nook she has a notoriety for
non-virtue. On the surface Evadne seems frail and fragile
yet she enjoys a reputation among the bloods of the
district. I have had a couple of near misses with her
myself as previously related.

This tale however only touches on Misses Menage
and Nook rather than being about them. The school

144

takes children up to the age of eleven. After that the youngsters move to Severnside Comprehensive or to a college of their parents' choice. There must be something about Severnham air or a certain isolation due to our living down by the river. Whatever it is, we enjoy the highest birthrate in the county. Babies all too soon grow into children needing to be educated. Regularly the village school entrants exceed places available.

Something had to be done and the education authorities came up with the following solution. Severnham Village School would be enlarged to include an extra class at a higher grade. This meant a headteacher coming to take charge and a new house being built for him. Before I go on with the Romeo and Juliet story, here is a little more information about the new head teacher, Kenneth Betterman, together with his wife Marjorie.

Kenneth is one of those forty-something types who look as they did at fourteen. His fair head of hair remains thick and tousled. His light blue eyes appear innocent of this wicked world. His voice is boyish and slightly high pitched in a refined sort of way.

Elizabeth Spinks, a shrewd judge of people, summed Kenneth up as a weak character.

'Heaven preserve us from those,' she added. 'Believe me, they are the worse.'

Marjorie does not enter much into this tale. I mention her in passing because she is the kind of woman who is anathema to modern feminists. Marjorie genuinely believes males are the natural masters of females and wives exist to bear their husband's babies. She is also a non-coper, unable to manage her present three and dreading the fourth on the way.

Anyway – or 'anyroad' as Gloucestershire folk would

say – the Bettermans moved into their new house. Misses Menage and Nook made them welcome. Our vicar and his wife did the same. Dorothy was as helpful to Marjorie as to everyone else. The rest of Severnham reserved judgement. I recalled Elizabeth's remark and felt something interesting might develop. None of us had long to wait.

Within a week of the Betterman's arrival, notices appeared on all the village boards. They were headed 'Severnham Players' and read,

'Have you a hidden talent for acting and stagecraft? Find out by joining the Severnham Players. Come to our first meeting on Friday evening at 7.30 in the Church Hall.' The notices were signed 'Kenneth Betterman. Director/Actor/Manager'.

There was a notice in the village store and that is the one I saw. Edward Spinks watched me read it then remarked,

'Our new head teacher seems to be a man of many parts.'

'I'm all for creative people,' I said. 'Severnham could do with an amateur dramatic society. Help pass the winter months.'

'In the Home Counties,' Elizabeth laughed, 'such societies were refuges for the randy.'

'And I was thinking of going . . . '

'You go and don't mind my spoilsport wife,' Edward said. 'Then you can tell us what transpires.'

I went and was surprised to see over twenty people, many of whom I did not know. The ones I recognised were Misses Menage and Nook; Arthur Tremblett from the council; sisters Janis and Jackie, who were I am sure,

146

there for the laughs, and Robin Pender the limp-wristed trainee chef at The Restoration.

We were all glancing uneasily at each other when Kenneth, carrying a clipboard, hurried into the hall. He wore a short-sleeved shirt with a bright flowered pattern and pink trousers.

'Good evening everyone,' he said, leaping lightly on to the platform. 'I'm Kenneth Betterman who you will be privileged henceforth to call Ken. Obviously you are all interested in the dramatic art because you are here. I hope to foster that. It will mean hard work. On the other hand it can be fun.

'Tonight,' he went on, 'we are going to do two things. The first is to fill in these forms.' Ken waved a batch of papers at us. 'The second is for each of you to mount this stage and read a few lines to the rest. All right? Good, good.'

Before anyone could think of anything to say, Ken leapt down and began handing out forms. The questionnaire was simple and one sided – name, address and telephone number; job, hobbies and other interests; previous acting experience (if any) and the types of roles we might wish to tackle.

People dutifully began filling in their forms. I was next to Arthur Tremblett, our District Surveyor and general slave to Chief Councillor Conrad Twist. To my surprise I saw him write the following words in the last section of the form. 'Masterful types.' Arthur caught me reading and remarked,

'I did quite a lot of amateur dramatics in my youth.'

'Really?'

'Oh yes.'

'What sort of roles have you played?'

'Well,' said Arthur, 'I am remembered for my Caesar. And particularly my Tamburlaine.'

Next came the readings. They were obviously Shakespeare, but to my shame I did not recognise a single one. Ken had them typed on different sheets of paper with no titles. The first went to Arthur Tremblett who grew in stature as he mounted the stage and began,

'Rebellious subjects, enemies to peace. Profaners of this neighbour-stained steel. Will they not hear . . ? '

Golly, I thought, Arthur is showing us how. Jackie and Janis, suppressing their giggles behind me, in no way diminished his performance.

After Arthur came Miss Menage. She was handed a piece of paper and read,

'There's no trust. No faith. No honesty in men. All perjured. All dissemblers . . . '

Miss Menage did well, perhaps because she was a teacher, and Miss Nook quite well. Her little voice whispered,

'It is the lark that sings so out of tune, straining harsh discords and unpleasant sharps . . . '

I should know that, I kept thinking, then it was my turn to go on the platform. The lines given me were in verse. 'Patience perforce with wilful choler meeting. Makes my flesh tremble in their different greeting. I will withdraw, but this intrusion shall. Now seeming sweet, convert to bitter gall.'

I thought I had not done badly until Robin Pender from The Restoration was given the same lines to read.

The assistant chef, standing centre stage, changed from a diffident person into a chill and menacing character. His voice was cold as he read the same lines.

148

Moreover he pronounced the word 'choler' correctly, which was more than I had done.

'He's good,' Arthur Tremblett said to me.

'What's the part?'

'Tybalt. All the quotations are from *Romeo and Juliet*. Mine's the Prince of Verona. Miss Menage the Nurse. Miss Nook Juliet . . . though I don't think she'll get the part.'

'Why not?'

'Well,' Arthur Tremblett gave a knowing chuckle, 'do I have to spell it out?'

'I don't think I'm going to get mine either.'

'No,' he agreed. I was seeing a different Tremblett from the person our Chief Councillor daily used to vilify.

Let me hasten over my ignominy so as to get on with the main story. After the first tests, Kenneth Betterman drew me to one side and asked if I had done any stagehand work? I replied no, but did not mind helping in any way possible. This cleared the air. Ken then went on to Miss Nook.

'Sorry Evadne. Good try, but I can't quite see you as Juliet.'

'I understand, Mr Betterman.'

'Ken please. Please call me Ken out of school.'

Although he did not actually tell us, we gathered the part of Romeo would be played by boyish Ken Betterman. As the search for his Juliet went on, he began to fit other characters into their chosen roles. Miss Menage became a kindly Nurse, Robin Pender a ruthless Tybalt and Arthur Tremblett a stern Prince. The last did not hesitate to put lesser beings, such as stagehands, in their place. Miss Nook was appointed prompter, also under-

149

study for Juliet – if such a wondrous being could be found in Severnham.

The search for Juliet was long and well noted around the district. It spread from Severnham, Twiggleswood and Lesser Sodham along the loop. Notices were even put up at Severnside Comprehensive School and similar establishments, containing it was hoped, a suitable virgin.

She arrived one afternoon to collect her two boys from the village school. Ken Betterman, who was talking to another parent, rudely broke off the conversation and rushed over to Sue, pretty wife of Basher Fluke. Sue had remained slim after the two births. Her dark hair shone like a burnished helmet. Her face was one of utter serenity when she was not arguing with her husband or lashing out at the boys. Like those of the other Flukes, hers was a very physical family.

'Er, excuse me,' Ken said, 'but I haven't seen you around before.' To which Sue replied,

'I was born in Severnham and have lived here all my life.'

'I meant here. At the school.'

'My two know their way home,' Sue informed Ken, 'but this afternoon they're due at the dentist. That's why I've arrived. Before they vanished.'

About half a dozen other mums did not seem to be listening to this conversation, but had noted every word. These were duly spread through Severnham which was how I heard. The exchange went as follows.

'I'd . . . er, like to have a talk with you,' Ken said. 'Is it possible for you to come back here. After the dentist?'

'After the dentist,' Sue told him, 'I have to fill them and my husband up with tea and wads.'

'Oh yes. I see. May I walk along with you then?'

'Sure. Come on boys! Your head teacher's going to keep us company. You'd better be on your best behaviour.'

During the short walk from the school to the health centre, I am assuming Ken talked to Sue about the role of Juliet. At the dentist they had to wait and other mums there reported further words. Sue was heard to say,

'Get away with you!'

'I mean it.'

'Me? Play Juliet?'

'You could.'

'You're pulling my leg, Mr Betterman.'

'No I'm not. You have the potential, Sue . . . '

The Severnham Players' production of *Romeo and Juliet* began with twice weekly readings. For the first fortnight Sue Fluke did not appear and, in my humble capacity as stagehand, I wondered whether our leading lady would be available. Miss Nook her understudy hoped, but we knew otherwise. Country people enjoy sources of information undreamed of by townies.

As I mentioned, Sue is married to Basher Fluke. Her cousin Vera Fluke works at Spinks store. In addition, Vera's younger sister Kate has a delicatessen at the shop. And, if that is not enough, there are Vera and Kate's brothers, Fred and Des – pals of Basher – on the newspaper delivery side. In other words, the rest of us had four information sources concerning Sue.

According to Vera, Basher choked on his faggots when he heard Sue had been asked to play Juliet. According to Kate, Sue's two tough little lads were ashamed of her having anything to do with Old Bedwetter. In the cases of Fred and Des, they darkly hinted it was about time Mr Betterman paid attention to Mrs Betterman.

But fate tends to have a hand in these matters and Sue turned up for the fifth reading. Everyone else looked on patiently while Ken made a fuss of her and a fool of himself.

'Here is your script, darling. By the way,' he hurriedly continued, 'everyone calls each other darling in the theatrical world. About the script, our reading it together will help you to memorise it.'

'I'll never learn all this.' Sue looked doubtfully at the script.

'It's my shortened version,' Ken informed her. 'I've cut surplus characters and scenes.'

'Can you do that?'

'I've done it!' Ken sounded like a bragging boy.

'What I mean is,' Sue persisted, 'is it all right? I don't want to do anything wrong.'

Janis and Jackie as Ladies Montague and Capulet dissolved into shrieks of laughter.

'I do!' cried Janis.

'Given half the chance,' Jackie agreed.

'It's perfectly all right, darling,' Ken reassured Sue. 'Shakespeare's plays have been cut, expanded, performed in modern dress. They are of infinite variety. Like Cleopatra.'

'I thought we were doing *Romeo and Juliet*.'

'I'm just quoting to make a point. Age cannot wither her, nor custom stale her infinite variety. Love poetry, the finest of which is in *Romeo and Juliet*.'

'Got it?' Miss Nook asked Sue rather tartly.

'If you say so . . . ' Sue said to Ken. 'I thought Shakespeare was . . . well, a kind of national heritage.'

'He is, darling. He is. But it is common practice to take liberties with Will.'

Ladies Montague and Capulet again dissolved into laughter.

Such was the background to the Shakespearean activities of the Severnham Players. I suppose our experiences followed those of most amateur theatricals. Some participants, like Arthur Tremblett and Robin Pender, were no problem. Others like the Ladies Montague and Capulet were made to suppress their mirth. In my case I was promoted from stagehand to manager because there was no one else. It became my responsibility to convert the church hall stage into fair Verona.

I was mentally listing the impossibilities when Dottie Mead looked in to see how we were coping. This prompted me to seek her help. Despite the nickname, Dottie was both practical and learned. She had read History at Oxford, which was more than the rest of us had done. So I put my problem to her.

'False arches,' she promptly replied.

'Pardon?'

'Cut arches out of hardboard and fit them about a foot from the back wall. Paint everything matt white and have two sets of lights – spots upfront and floods concealed behind the arch columns. In that way you can simulate scenes from sunrise to sunset, also all through the night.'

'Dottie, you're brilliant!'

'And you must have a balcony.'

'What . . . ?'

'Romeo looks up at it. Juliet looks down from it. Famous love scene. Remember?'

'Ah yes. Perhaps I could manage the arches, but a balcony is beyond me.'

'Essential nevertheless,' Dottie emphasised. 'We don't want Sue giving her all on a collapsing balcony.'

The stage manager decided to sub-contract the arches (incorporating a balcony) and the electrics. It was put out to tender – well, I asked around the village. Two Flukes got the jobs. There was Phil the electrician I had used before and his kid brother Wayne who had taken a Youth Opportunity course in carpentry. Phil said to me in that confidential voice of his,

'Means we can keep an eye on our Sue.'

We are only human in Severnham, which is another way of saying we are nosy. The main item of interest at the twice weekly rehearsals was how Ken would set about transforming Sue into Juliet. The rest of us, while carrying out our duties, kept a spare eye and ear trained in their direction.

'You must understand,' Ken told Sue, 'we are utterly besotted by each other.'

'You mean on the stage?'

'It's more than that, Sue. You have to get into the part so you feel it every waking hour.'

'Like I fancy you?'

'It goes beyond fancy. I am talking about first love. An emotion which envelops you. Takes you over. Leads you to . . . to you don't know where.'

'Cor!' breathed Sue.

'I'm serious.' Suddenly Ken seemed to realise what he had taken on. 'Listen to me, darling. Shakespeare wrote some of the finest love poetry the world has ever known. You are privileged to learn, to speak, to re-enact his sacred words.'

154

'In that case,' Sue retorted, 'you should never have chopped them.'

'I didn't chop those!' Ken's high pitch voice rose to a strangulated squeak. 'The love scenes – your lines and mine – are unabridged. Come on, let's go though the balcony scene again and try to get it right this time.'

As narrator of how Severnham Players put on *Romeo and Juliet*, I may seem to be mocking them. Let me therefore try and make amends by recording their considerable efforts. Sue, a simple country girl, learned her lines not only by heart, but what they meant. She became word perfect and followed Ken's direction to the letter. Other Flukes also worked wonders.

At this point I should emphasise how the Flukes are practical people. Their creativity may be a bit primitive, yet they make up for it by a stubborn resolve to do their best. Sue and her female relatives worked long and hard at the costumes she would be wearing. Similarly the Fluke lads, Phil and Wayne, constructed an excellent set with elegant arches (incorporating a balcony) and sky lighting effects ranging from sunny Italian days to passionate star-filled nights.

Reports about these efforts rippled round the district. There were many points of local interest. Strong rumour had it that Arthur Tremblett's Prince of Verona was based on Chief Councillor Conrad Twist. The villagers called this 'Arthur's Revenge'. They also heard about spectacular sword play (true), costume rivalry between Janis and Jackie (untrue) and sizzling love scenes between Ken and our Sue as the star-crossed lovers (Oh ah). It all made for good publicity.

By then the play had reached the late rehearsal stages – four full ones and two dress rehearsals. I must say this for Kenneth Betterman, he was thorough and insistent. We were now moving towards the opening night when, according to theatrical lore, 'it would be all right'. Every ticket had been sold for the first performance on Thursday evening and most seats taken for Friday and Saturday.

Country performances may not have the grandeur of those in big cities, but they do enjoy plenty of local hype. The main attractions were to see how 'he' or 'she' got on and of course what 'her' was wearing. Every entrance and exit, every word and gesture, especially any mistake, would be instantly noted and endlessly discussed.

Let me say – before I describe the two things which went wrong – that the performances were to the highest professional standards. Every player looked good and acted well. The local rag even mentioned me and my set.

Readers may recall that Sue is married to Basher Fluke who repairs agricultural machinery. A gentle giant doing a dirty job, Basher has his workshop next to the bungalow which Sue tries in vain to keep clean. Her task is a hard one, what with Basher and their two thug-like kids.

On the afternoon before the first night, Sue and sisters sat making last minute alterations to one of her costumes. They were nearly done when the boys arrived home from school. As usual the kids were ravenous. They kept on saying so to their mother and aunts until each thug was given a sticky bun.

While eating his bun, the youngest boy tried fingering the costume and was pushed away by the nearest aunt. At that moment, Basher came in for his tea. It presented an opportunity which his son immediately seized. The soft push was upgraded to a hard blow.

Basher himself had had a hard day. The bent axle from one of Tiny Palmer's tractors broke during straightening and Basher knew Tiny would not pay for a new one. So Sue's husband was already annoyed when he arrived for tea. There he found his wife and her sisters fussing over dresses 'for that sodding play'. Moreover, Basher thought Sue had hit his son.

'Why did you thump him?' Basher wanted to know.

'Never did,' retorted Sue.

'I pushed him out of the way,' Sue's sister intervened. 'He tried to touch the dress with his sticky fingers.'

This was the point when Basher blew. He had suffered a great deal over the preceding weeks. His wife had been caught up in the play. His home life was disrupted. His family and friends, especially those at The Piggy, kept pulling his leg. In the circumstances, what he said could be called mild.

'I'll be glad when the bloody play's over.'

Which was the point when Sue blew. She too had been under stress and was, at that moment, afflicted by first night nerves. Her outburst took two forms, starting with words.

'That's typical of you,' Sue yelled at Basher. 'You don't begin to understand what I have been through. What I have tried to do. All you know are your home comforts, bacon sandwiches and pints down at The Piggy.' With that Sue attacked Basher.

According to the Flukes who work for Edward and Elizabeth Spink at the village store, Sue and Basher often have dust-ups. She likes to fling blows that Basher easily deflects. With his strength, Basher could pick Sue up and break her in two, but her attacks generally make him laugh. Vera Fluke used a lovely expression about such scenes.

'They're like a doe attacking a bull elephant.'

Normally the spats soon end with kisses and cuddles, following which the boys are told to go out and play. This time however Sue began delivering some real blows, Basher tried to grab her hands and one huge heavy paw slipped past hers to hit Sue in the eye.

Pandemonium followed. The sisters and sons accused Basher of attacking Sue. Sue said it was her fault. Basher tried to comfort her. The sisters rushed around searching for a steak to put on Sue's eye, but all anyone had were deep frozen ones. They tried towels soaked in cold water to no avail. All too soon the black eye was clearly visible.

Meanwhile time was ticking by. Sue had to be at the church hall at six. She arrived distraught accompanied by her husband, boys, sisters and a large contingent of Flukes. Fortunately the first person they met was Dottie.

'Evadne Nook'll have to take over,' wailed Sue.

'Nonsense!' Dottie said sharply.

'Look at it.' Sue removed the face flannel she was now holding to her black eye.

'Haven't you heard of stage make-up?' asked Dottie. 'I'll do it for you myself.'

Dottie told me later she had never handled stage make-up in her life. However circumstances called for it. As she applied cream then powder, the vicar's wife spoke soothingly to Sue.

'The show must go on, as they say. It is the sign of a true professional.'

'But I'm not a professional,' sniffed Sue. 'I'm just me.'

'For goodness sake, stop snivelling! Your eye is looking quite normal, so don't you go and ruin it.'

'Thanks Dottie,' Sue said and they hugged each other.

I have previously mentioned how the dressing room part of the church hall is minimal. Dottie had attended to Sue in the general dressing room while Kenneth Betterman, as actor manager and star, had the other cubby hole. In the foyer, beyond the short narrow passage leading to the two rooms, a small group of Flukes had gathered with Basher in their midst. He was unhappy at having harmed his Sue, also causing problems for the play.

'You ought to go and apologise to Mr Betterman,' the Fluke women insisted.

'You should, Dad,' the Fluke boys agreed.

So Basher levered his way along the narrow passage and knocked on Ken's door. He was not to know that actor managers and even stars also suffer from first night nerves.

'What is it?' Ken asked of Basher.

'Come to apologise for what happened to my Sue.'

'A little too late,' Ken snapped.

'I didn't mean it.'

'They all say that.'

'Who . . . ?' Basher ponderously enquired.

'Oafs like you.' Slim, short boyish Ken – dressed in his Romeo outfit – stood up and confronted big beefy Basher. 'You have no idea what is going on here. How difficult, how plucky it is for a person like Sue to tackle such a part. She is a lovely creature and you . . . you're just like a great big ape with . . . with a Stradivarius violin.'

The Fluke family and members of the cast, who were crowded in the corridor to hear this altercation, thought Basher would either shake or crush Ken to death. All they could see was Basher's back as his vast frame held open the sprung door to the star's dressing room. They heard Basher repeat the apology then begin to reverse into the passage.

At that point there was some panic. The Fluke family had to back towards the foyer or be crushed themselves. At the same time the cast were obliged to withdraw into the other dressing room. It was a complicated manoeuvre, particularly as everyone present wanted to know what was happening up front.

Because of the confusion, no one actually witnessed the key event – though it was much discussed afterwards. As Basher retreated, still mumbling his apologies, Ken advanced angrily to shut the door which was already shutting. To tell what took place next in the simplest way, he walked into the end of the door. Sue had been inadvertently hit in the left eye. Now Ken suffered the same with his right.

Further pandemonium followed. Ken was crying with pain and frustration. Basher was all apologies. The onlookers were all agog. What had taken place was swiftly relayed to Sue. In an oblique way this helped to save the night. Dottie, who was still with Sue, went to deal with Ken. As she struggled past, Dottie kept shouting to everyone,

'Out! Out! Out!'

Following the best theatrical tradition, the show did go on. The important people arrived, led by the Twists, to occupy the front row. As stage manager I kept to one side, near to the Meads and the Spinks. A solid block of Flukes stood across the back of the hall.

The curtains parted. Fair Verona, depicted by three arches and one balcony, was revealed. Arthur Tremblett, promoted from district surveyor to royal prince, addressed five citizens who shuffled their feet and looked contrite.

'Rebellious subjects, enemies to peace.'

We were on our way. All too soon Romeo was gazing up at the balcony and Juliet had appeared on it. More by luck than judgement, my balcony was left stage. This enabled the lovers to hide their disfigurements – Sue's left eye and Ken's right – by keeping profiles to the audience.

And then I forgot even that. The magic of Shakespeare's words and the dedication of pretty little Sue Fluke captivated us all. She was no longer the wife of Basher and the mother of two tough boys, but a maiden again, bewildered by first love.

'O gentle Romeo. If thou dost love, pronounce it faithfully. Or if you think'st I am too quickly won, I'll frown and be perverse and say thee nay.'

Her anguished voice moved us all.

Best Seller

On previous occasions I have mentioned a house named The Grange which stands diagonally across the lane from my cottage. It is regarded by the villagers as an unlucky place and there has been a turnover of people living in it. Built originally for our chief councillor, he soon moved to a higher home on Severnham Hill. Then followed a succession of short stay residents such as a Foreign Office family, a brother and sister from Hong Kong, a group of red-headed call girls and a charity organiser whose bonfire party caused a much larger blaze.

The Twists who own The Grange have other family interests including estate, development and construction companies. These are run by Jason, eldest son of Chief Councillor Conrad Twist. Tall, superior and a younger version of his father, I just about manage to get on with him. The trick is to let Jason portray his superior self. Thus I mentally made the allowance on the spring morning when he stopped at my cottage.

'You'll soon be having a new neighbour,' Jason told me.

'Oh really?' Another trick is not to appear interested. Jason Twist might have been born rich and had a Cheltenham Boys College education, but he was still a Gloucestershire person.

'Someone famous,' he hinted.

'That'll be nice,' I said, so he drip fed a little more.

'A best selling novelist.'

'Interesting.'

'Her books sell in millions.'

'People tend to talk millions these days,' I said.

At last Jason realised I was sending him up. He nodded, grunted and left.

The outcome of all this was that the latest occupant at The Grange would be one Felicity Copeland. I had heard the name, but never read any of her books. As for the house, it was not blessed with her presence for some time due to Twist workmen making alterations. The interval allowed our local grapevine to obtain advance information, mostly from the librarian.

'Oh yes,' she told me, 'a surprising number of people have asked about Copeland. In fact, all her books are out at the moment.'

'What are they like?'

'In my opinion, Felicity Copeland has a single plot, which she uses every year, though the settings vary. She has written seventeen novels, but you only need to read one.'

'Tell me the plot.'

'She uses a simple theme appealing to more than half the human race. Her heroine is always a woman much put upon by men. Halfway through the book she meets a man who seems to be the one she has been waiting for, but of course he's no good. After a session of ingenious carnality, usually in Chapter 18, she repudiates him and puts her life together again. End of book.'

Felicity Copeland duly arrived. She was accompanied by another woman and they kept to themselves in the house. As usual, Edward Spinks was the first to call and become their grocer. After Edward delivered a big box of groceries to The Grange, he brought me my usual weekly order. Edward and I were once Londoners, so I could ask him direct questions.

'What's she like?'

'The Copeland didn't deal with me. She has a secretary companion, Marion Harding, who looks after such matters. A pleasant though – I would say – a much put upon person.'

'Surely you saw them both?'

'No, only Marion. Well educated. Middle aged. Sensible. The great authoress did not put in an appearance.'

'Well, here's a picture of her.' I produced the novel Mrs Hands had booked out to me. The back cover showed a halo-haired woman with an enigmatic smile staring at the camera. She had a long neck.

'We have the same picture on the one we actually bought. Her last novel which was Booker-listed.'

'Have you read it?'

'Elizabeth has.'

'What does she think?'

'She says it's all surface sheen. Written to be read by females with the mental age of twelve. My dear wife can be devastating at times.'

A few days went by before Marion Harding began her long walks. At first I caught glimpses of her at a distance. She wore tweeds and sensible shoes. Later she came past my place and replied to 'good mornings' from the Hopskips and me. Marion Harding then began visiting the village shop and occasionally going to church.

Our first real meeting and conversation took place on the hill. I too had gone for a walk and came upon her rounding a corner of the wood. From close-up I was able to notice more. Women's ages are a total mystery to me, but I would guess early fifties. Marion had retained a slim athletic figure and she walked briskly. Her face was pleasant though somewhat sad. However the main impressions were the dark pupils of her eyes and a precise voice.

To my surprise, when we reached the final stretch of the lane, she invited me into The Grange for a cup of tea. I said something about not wishing to disturb the authoress. To this Marion replied,

'You won't see her. She's working.'

'All the more reason . . . '

'She's working in her attic suite.'

Over tea in the kitchen, Marion explained. Felicity had an attic room built with a large window looking towards Severnham Hill. There were eating, washing and sleeping facilities so the authoress could remain undisturbed for days and nights on end.

No sooner had she told me this than a voice called from the top of the stairs.

'Marion!'

'Yes? Excuse me.' Marion went to the door.

'Did you process the last chapter?'

'Yes. It's on the cabinet.'

'I didn't see it.'

'It's there.'

A long silence followed with Marion remaining by the door. Eventually she returned to where we were sitting and said,

'Felicity must have found it or she would have called back to me. More tea?'

Over a second cup, Marion told how Felicity's novels were written. The gestation period went on for months before pen could be put to paper. During that time the authoress was restless. Reference works had to be obtained. Sudden journeys made. Some were as far afield as India and South America.

'After that,' said Marion, 'she writes with a felt tip pen on half sheets. Some are discarded and rewritten. A day's work will be two to three thousand words. Felicity then either gives the bundle of half sheets to me or leaves them on a cabinet outside her attic suite. I wordprocess the manuscripts and either hand the copies to her or leave them on the cabinet.'

'Sounds simple enough,' I commented.

'Well, we do have our little crises.'

Felicity Copeland and Marion Harding lived at The Grange for three and a half years. No sooner had they arrived than the bad luck factor of the house was applied to the authoress.

Instead of reviewing her latest novel, a London journalist – the kind called investigative – took Felicity Copeland apart. He went through her potted biography and dealt with each entry as follows. Born in Bedford-shire (Luton). Had a convent school education (Expelled). Learned her craft (Dropped out). First novel accepted (Lived with first publisher). It was nasty stuff yet no one in Severnham took the slightest notice.

As for Marion Harding, she once told me her father was a rector and her mother had died shortly after her birth. Later Marion went up to Newnham and into publishing. Later still she heard Felicity Copeland wanted a secretary companion, applied for and had held down the job ever since.

It was not easy work. Felicity proved to be a difficult employer. The authoress did whatever she wanted regardless of everyone else. Suddenly she might decide to visit Bangkok or Rio. She argued with her agent, publisher and others in the literary world as if they were cretins. A large imperious woman, Felicity had discarded two husbands as well as what she called loose guns. In popular parlance she did not give a damn.

Yet this set-up, seemingly remote from village activities, would cause the greatest changeover to take place at Severnham since the Restoration. It all happened indirectly.

Marion at The Grange was in complete charge of the house and garden. She managed very well despite her main duties as a secretary companion. However Marion worried about the garden because come the spring everything would start to grow. During their first summer she mowed the lawns and weeded the beds, but clearly more work was needed. Shortly before the year end, which Felicity Copeland had decreed they were to spend in Morocco, Marion asked me who might help her with the garden.

167

'There are outside gardening services,' I replied, 'and here there are the Flukes.'

'I rather like the sound of the Flukes.'

'They're all right,' I said. 'Honest in their own way and hard working. Cheaper as well.'

'How can I contact them?'

'Let me do it for you. Their chief is Garnet Fluke . . . '

'Garnet,' said Marion. 'What a lovely name.'

Accordingly I visited The Boar's Head and saw Garnet in his usual chair by a blazing log fire. Charlie Fluke the church gravedigger was with him and several younger Flukes. A round of drinks provided a convivial atmosphere.

When I told Garnet about Marion's request, he nodded, but did not reply for the moment. This was what I expected. As for the young Flukes, they laughed and began speculating on the relationship of 'them two women at The Grange'. There were many knowing chuckles and a great many 'Oh ahs'.

Suddenly Garnet said in a growly sort of voice,

'Let's have no more of that talking about ladies.'

There was instant silence during which Garnet told me he would call on Miss Harding at nine next morning. 'If it suits?'

He did call though I did not hear the outcome straight away as Felicity and Marion were leaving for Morocco. On their return the authoress ascended to her ivory tower while Marion took up the running of The Grange as if she had never left. Come to think of it, I never heard anything about the various places they used to visit.

When I next saw Marion – in late January – she told me about Garnet Fluke's visit.

'An amazing man,' Marion said.

'In what way?'

'I mean he's a one-off.'

'Garnet's that,' I agreed.

'So knowledgeable about plants. I bought myself a potted poinsettia and azalea for Christmas. When I remarked to Garnet Fluke it was a pity neither would last, he replied they could go on for years.

'Mine always die back,' Marion told him.

'Because of them wicked garden centre people,' he told her. There and then he repotted the azalea to let it grow and, in the case of the poinsettia, removed a little plastic cage from around its roots.

During the rest of that winter, Garnet Fluke visited The Grange every other day. He kept Marion's poinsettia flamboyant and the freed azalea flourishing. He also arranged for a pair of young Flukes to look after the garden from the first day of spring.

After that, Garnet would pay regular visits and Marion often remarked to me,

'He's such a knowledgeable man, not only about gardens, but on other country matters. I pick his brains like mad.'

So Marion found an unexpected ally in Garnet Fluke, while Felicity continued to write cut off from the rest of Severnham. I wondered how true to life her characters could be, yet her books were popular and sold everywhere.

During work lunch hours, I would stroll from my Cheltenham office in Imperial Square to W. H. Smith and Waterstones on The Promenade. Both invariably had special stands displaying 'The latest Felicity Copeland'. Once some school girls, in a uniform not unknown locally, were giggling over what looked like a Chapter

18. When I mentioned this to Marion, she simply said, 'The cheques keep coming in.'

I must now move to the turning point, not only in the lives of Felicity and Marion, but also that of Severnham. The authoress had an agent who handled her public relations. This person was instructed to lay on a publicity occasion every three months. At least.

Marion told me these had included well-publicised book signings, a series of lectures for the Cheltenham Literary Festival and being 'Writer in Residence' at Gloucester.

'This time,' Marion said, 'she's going to have a forty minute television programme. Here in Severnham.'

Being Felicity Copeland, arrangements were made well in advance. The best-selling authoress decided to show her rapport with village life. There were to be shots of her strolling from The Grange towards the church. On the way Felicity would pause for a chat with a couple of locals.

'Would you,' Marion asked with a straight face, 'like to be one of them?'

'Who's the other?' I played for time.

'The vicar. Andrew Mead. He's agreed to be near the lych gate as Felicity approaches. They'll exchange a few words then he'll show her round the church. Apparently churches are very photogenic.'

'Well, I'm not. What sort of part did she have for me?'

'Digging in the garden with the cottage behind you. It's the cottage she wants really. Felicity will wave and call out to you. You've only to wave and call back.'

'Oh ah as they say round here.'

'The camera will be retreating as she advances. I believe they call it a tracking shot. Do help us. Please.'

'All right. If that's the extent of it.'

The news that 'the telly people' had arrived went round Severnham in a flash. They were staying at The Restoration and all reports put their number in two figures. Polly looked after them and I quote her words.

'We've been invaded by the scruffiest bunch ever at the inn. Dressed in expensive casuals, but dirty, worn and ill-fitting. They consider themselves superior. They're never on time for meals. They drink far too much. And what goes on upstairs, we'll never know.'

'Who are they, Polly? Sort them out for me.'

'Let's start with Flammetta . . . '

'Who?'

'Flammetta Smith. Literary Agent. Large lady with the gaudy clothes and loud voice. She handles everything. Or is supposed to. The others do what they want. Next comes the interviewer Dominic Nelmes. He of the golden corduroy outfit. Tousled haired – I don't think he has ever put a comb through it. Only his dirty fingers. Oh, his whispering voice! It's as if he's half asleep, but still so clever and insinuating.'

'Who's the tall, lantern-jawed one?'

'That's Jake the producer. Yorkshire born and bred. He's the one to watch. No one knows what he is going to do next. Half-mad if you ask me. The girl with the high chest is Pidge. His assistant and bed comforter. Those are the main four . . . '

'How many more?'

'Eight I think. Let me try and run through them. There's Art on Camera 1 and Sharma on Camera 2. Flakey handles Sound with Mavis. Then there are two technicians, two drivers and . . . no, that's the lot. In the evening, the main four sit near here and the rest go to the end of the room. You ought to look in and see for yourself.'

I did and saw what Polly meant. Never mind, I said to her. They'll only be here for a day or two.

The television people were in Severnham for over a week. To begin with their time was spent at The Grange photographing it from all angles, also the approaches and the outlook towards the hill. After that came Dominic Nelmes interviewing Felicity Copeland. Several sessions were conducted at different places to provide variety when editing. Once I saw them in the garden being tracked up and down the length of the lawn.

The next stage began when Pidge hurried over and asked me to start digging in front of my cottage.

'What would you wear for digging?' she asked.

'Oh, anything.'

'Jake wants something typically country,' she insisted, 'and would you roll up your sleeves?'

I put on a check cotton shirt, rolled up the sleeves, took out a spade and waited for the next two and a half hours. I was in the cottage when Pidge came hurrying back to say,

'We're ready.'

I went outside again to see the television people coming down the lane. In addition, lined up across the road, were many village people. The Hopskips, Samuel and Evangeline, stood in their garden watching as well – he with his collarless shirt, she wearing her apron and curlers.

But the funniest sight of all was Felicity Copeland. I had not realised before she was one of those unfortunate women with a box for hips and thick legs. This of course was not her fault and a shame really because the top half had presence and poise. There was another aspect. To date Felicity had totally ignored her garden and village activities. Now she wore a new pair of gardening gloves and carried a trugful of flowers for dressing the church.

'All I want you to do, Felicity,' Jake told her, 'is to keep on walking and wave at the man in the cottage garden as you go past. All I want you to do,' he turned to me, 'is to pause in your digging, smile and wave back.' The television man then called across to the Hopskips. 'Would you mind keeping out of the picture?'

Samuel and Evangeline did not move.

'Would you please . . . ?' Pidge went over to them.

'Our garden,' said Samuel.

'Oh ah,' Evangeline confirmed it.

There followed a terse confrontation between Jake and the Hopskips, with the latter winning in the end.

'I never thought this was a good idea,' Jake returned and told Flammetta. 'Probably I'd have cut it out in the editing.'

'I never thought it a good idea either.' Felicity thrust the trug, followed by her gardening gloves, at Flammetta who in turn gave them to Pidge. 'Let's go and talk to the vicar.'

With that the whole party trooped past me and my moment of fame never materialised.

'Mad lot,' said Samuel.

'Oh ah,' Evangeline agreed.

Andy Mead had been hovering in and around the church for most of the morning. I noticed he was wearing a grey outfit and dog collar. He greeted the approaching party, most of whom ignored him while they studied photo angles.

The resultant programme did not include the se-

173

quence with Andy and Felicity, though shooting took up the rest of the day. On the evening the programme went out, there was not a person to be seen in the village. I watched with the Meads and, after Andy had switched off, Dottie said,

'Well?'

She did not know what to say and neither did the rest of Severnham. For a start there was little about Felicity. She and Dominic had one session where he sleepily questioned her about 'physicality' in her novels. He smirked while asking,

'That passage where the Indian merchant advises your heroine on the Karma Sutra as physical exercises . . . '

More serious were the views of Felicity. The cameramen seemed to have shot her from every unflattering angle. Her hips and legs looked enormous.

'Cruel, cruel, cruel!' cried Dottie.

But there was worse to come. The 40-minute programme contained less than half about the authoress. The rest was made up of Garnet Fluke. Obviously, Jake the producer had become interested in Garnet's character and featured him to the detriment of Felicity.

'She's not going to be happy,' we all agreed.

This was confirmed next morning, a Saturday. I had got up later than usual and was setting about my weekend chores when there came a knock on the front door. To my surprise the caller turned out to be Marion Harding. She was formally dressed and a taxi cab stood outside. Marion extended her hand.

'I've come to say goodbye.'

'What do you mean? The broadcast . . . ?'

'Yes. Felicity has fired Flammetta. And me.'

174

'Why you?'

'It's too long and complicated.'

I insisted on her coming in and telling me while the cab driver waited.

'Felicity,' Marion explained, 'kept asking Flammetta for an advance view of the programme and Jake kept putting her off. Felicity blames Dominic. They've had words in the past.'

To recap what Marion told me, Felicity was leaving The Grange and going to stay temporarily at her London flat. It seems the vibes in Severnham had never been good.

'What about you?' I asked.

'Don't worry about me.'

'Have you anywhere to go?'

'A long-suffering brother in Yorkshire . . . until I sort out something else.'

'Are you sure?'

'Sure I'm sure.' Marion smiled. 'In fact I'm relieved. Felicity Copeland was never a comfortable person to live with. I get on well with my brother. He's in the woollen business. Very successful.'

'It was nice knowing you,' I said.

'And you.' Marion held out her hand once more. 'Can't keep the driver waiting any longer. Nice knowing you too. Maybe we'll meet again sometime.'

'I hope so.'

'You never know.'

I went to the garden gate and waved her off. Marion was being brave as well as polite. She would not, I wrongly thought, be returning to this backwater.

Felicity Copeland left Severnham the following afternoon without a backward glance. Later a large van called at The Grange – that unlucky house – to collect her belongings.

And yet the aftermath was far different from what everyone expected. Jake the television producer asked Garnet Fluke to participate in a series of six half-hour episodes of life around Severnham. Garnet said he would think about it, which resulted in the offer being raised.

'The question now is,' Edward Spink said to me, 'will money spoil the Flukes?'

For they were beginning to do quite well. Chris Fluke was running a successful computer business. The other Flukes were picking up an increasing amount of work, oddly enough, due to the recession. They undercut everyone else.

'Like true capitalists,' said Edward.

Eventually Jake persuaded Garnet to appear in the series. The television producer visited The Piggy, bought drinks all round and in the end Garnet agreed.

'So long as you don't try messing me about,' Garnet warned him.

'Would I do that?' Jake grinned. 'I'm a straight talking Yorkshireman – as you are a straight talking Gloucester-shire man.'

'Don't know anything about that there Yorkshire,' Garnet is reported to have said. 'And we don't go in for too much gabble in Gloucestershire.'

'Exactly what I'm looking for,' Jake told him.

'Oh ah,' Garnet replied.

Jake's series showed us another Severnham. The producer was quoted as saying, 'It's not what you put in, but what you leave out.' For example he left out our chief councillor and the rest of the Twists. The result

176

was a Severnham peopled by Flukes – grinning, knowing, unashamedly bucolic.

Our hill and woods formed an ever-present background. The patchwork fields were stitched together by living green hedges. The meadows were lush and packed with wild flowers. The river wound sinuously round the loop. Cattle and poultry, squirrels and rabbits, foxes and badgers appeared to be in communion with Garnet Fluke who handled and talked wisely about them.

It was Garnet's home which surprised me most of all. Up to then I had no idea where he lived and in what style. It was now revealed a cart track ran from behind The Boar's Head over a rise to Hunter's Lodge. In the old days the lodge had been used by hunters and Garnet's father the local gamekeeper lived in an outhouse. The place was surprisingly large to accommodate hunting parties and had plenty of ground filled with creatures great and small. Jake's film put this over wonderfully.

There was another surprise to come. The last episode of the series showed Garnet Fluke at home. It was a day in his Severnham life. How he rose at dawn to talk to and feed the animals. How he kept everything neat and tidy. How he went to The Piggy for a liquid lunch. Included in almost the last shot was a brief picture of Marion Harding.

'Good Lord!' I exclaimed when watching the last episode at the Meads. 'Was that . . . ?'

'It was,' Dottie smiled and Andy confirmed it.

'Severnham's best kept secret.'

'But I've never seen Marion Harding since she left The Grange. Never heard any more about her.'

'Let me explain,' said Andy. 'According to my grapevine, the television producer included her as a sort of in-joke. It seems he did not like Felicity Copeland, Flammetta Smith and PR-inspired programmes.'

'Why should a programme about Garnet include Marion?'

'Because,' Dottie clapped her hands, 'they're engaged.'

'Garnet and Marion?'

'Yes.' Andy confirmed a second time. 'Garnet's a widower. His first wife died early in the marriage. Marion is a spinster. While he was looking after the garden at The Grange, she got on very well with him. They found much in common. Since then they have corresponded . . . '

'Garnet writes a beautiful copperplate,' Dottie told me.

I kept shaking my head and saying,

'Garnet and Marion engaged?'

'Yes.' Andy gave his third confirmation. 'I'll be marrying them soon.'

Which is what happened. It was not a grand affair, as with Edward and Elizabeth's daughter, but I felt it more typical of Severnham. There were no Twists of course and no grand guests, but the Flukes put on a good show.

The Fluke men wore their best dark suits with fresh white carnations in every buttonhole. The Fluke women surprised me with their fineries. Their thuggish lads and tomboyish girls were scrubbed three times and forced into new outfits. As for Garnet and Marion, they were – how can I put it – just right. He had on a charcoal grey suit with a white shirt and blue tie. She wore powder blue silk. They made a fine couple.

The Reverend Andrew Mead officiated. The vicar's

wife, Dorothy and their children attended, as did the Hopskips, the Clements, the Oakshotts and the Palmers. I kept feeling it was a genuine Severnham Village occasion. After the church ceremony, the photographs and the confetti, we went to a reception laid on in the cleared car park of The Boar's Head. There were white clothed trestle tables, catering tents and coloured lights in the trees. It was a happy event.

At the time, as I have previously mentioned, none of us realised how much this particular marriage would change local lives.

Woman in Grey

Meanwhile the Twists continued to reign supreme. I have mentioned how my office is in Imperial Square, Cheltenham. Across the gardens from me are the offices of Jason Twist. These contain his family companies on the estate, development and construction sides. Occasionally I bump into Jason and very occasionally we have a drink at lunch time. It allows him to drop hints about clever and influential deals.

Basically, Jason is an estate agent. He also possesses the financial means to acquire and develop suitable sites. In addition the family has what they call a construction company. This is a small building firm. It comprises a staff of two with the rest being sub-contracted labour.

Thus Jason's office is a front, but an impressive one. Wide steps ascend to the elegant entrance. The Regency rooms are well proportioned. Decorous furnishings and assistants greet visitors. Hospitality bestowed is in direct proportion to spending power expected.

I must say this for Jason, he has always been friendly to me in his lofty way. It was a lovely autumn day when he waved and introduced me to the gorgeous girl with him. She was tall, slim, athletic, with light golden hair cut short and eyes like aquamarines. I saw she had the Twist chin and manner.

'Meet Trisha,' Jason made the introduction. 'My sister.'

We went to a wine bar. As Jason said he would be using his American Express, I let him have the pleasure of ordering fresh salmon and something ridiculously expensive to drink. It left me free to feast my eyes on Trisha.

'How is it I've never seen you round here?' I asked her.

'I've been at our London office,' she told me.

'Didn't know you had one.'

'Now you do.' Trisha laughed, revealing small teeth.

'What happens at your London office?' I probed, with a side glance at Jason who was still ordering. 'Why have one?'

'There are two reasons,' Trisha crisply informed me. 'The trend is towards centralisation. These days London needs to know and London decides. It is best to be represented there. The other reason has to do with serious money. The City. Merchant banks. Fund holders. Foreign investors. So I did my stint in London before returning to Gloucestershire.'

I was beginning to see another Trisha. On the way back to my office, also on the drive home to Severnham, I kept thinking about her. Perhaps it was good to find a partner with feet on the financial ground. My fault was I am all too often up in the clouds. Floating aimlessly.

After that first meeting, I took to looking in at the Twist Cheltenham office around lunchtime. All too frequently Trisha was elsewhere, but when I saw her and suggested lunch she would smile and say in that cool voice of hers, 'Why not?'

I began going out with Trisha and, although she remained friendly and even loving, there were certain factors which gave me pause. For example she was prohibitively expensive to know. I would try to encourage her 'Why nots?', but at the end of a typical evening the total outlays were either nudging or into three figures.

'That's what attractive girls are for,' I kept telling myself while my other half would be warning me to 'watch it.'

Then there was the case of all too often seeing her with men she told me were 'clients'. They came in expensive business suits, sports clothes and country attire. They drove fabulous cars. They obviously had more money than me. I did not like asking Trisha who were they exactly, but after she had been away for a weekend, a week or longer I had to know.

Her replies were always unsatisfactory. Trisha would throw out single words or short remarks like 'Yachting', 'Skiing' or 'I was in the Caymans.' Clearly I was being outclassed.

What really settled the matter for me took the form of some stray remarks she made. We were talking about the main differences between living in London and the country. She said,

'The important lesson London taught me is always to win. I won't enter any relationship, business or otherwise, unless I am sure of winning. Once there, I'll do everything to win.'

'Like all's fair in love and war.'

'Fair or unfair,' said Trisha, 'I'll do it.'

I had not seen Trisha for some time as winter began to succeed autumn. Then one evening I looked into The Restoration and there she was with Jason and an elderly couple. I gave her a brief wave before turning to Polly behind the bar. Before I could place my order, Jason hurried over to me.

'What are you drinking?'

'It's all right . . . '

'I insist. Also you might like to meet the Eaglebergers.'

'The who?'

'Hiram King and Eleanor May Eagleberger.'

'Clients?'

'Very much so.'

I should have said no, but Trisha smiled whenever I looked her way. Apart from that, I cannot resist the temptation of new faces, characters, situations, stories.

As their names betrayed, the Eaglebergers were American. Just as clearly, the dominant partner was Eleanor May. A large woman, she took control of every conversation. While Jason tried to impress, Trisha simply sat back smiling and nodding. I thought this is the one deal the Twists are not going to win. In the case of Hiram King, he looked a little man with a blank face. Later I learned he was high up in the US Embassy and a pocket tyrant to his staff.

But why had Jason called me over? There could only be one reason. In some way, it was to help further Twist business.

I agreed because of Trisha's presence. She had said little, leaving Mrs Eagleberger to do all the talking. Over the next hour we heard about the Eagleberger's house in the Georgetown district of Washington DC; the Eagleberger family homes in Maryland and Virginia; the Eagleberger stud farm in Kentucky; the Eagleberger ocean cruiser kept moored at Annapolis and the Eagleberger's pokey little apartment in 'your Mayfair, London, England'. Eleanor May declared, 'We Americans like space.'

'Plenty of that at Twiggleswood Court,' said Jason, causing Trisha to frown slightly while continuing to smile.

'How did I get into this?' I asked her when the Americans decided to retire for the night and Jason went with them to the foot of the hotel staircase.

'You walked in,' she said, 'and Jason just did it. Heavy going here.'

'What are you doing next?'

'Back to Cheltenham with Jason.'

It had been arranged we meet in The Restoration at ten. I got up early, went to work for a couple of hours, then returned to Severnham. Jason and Trisha duly arrived. They let me travel in the Eagleberger's monstrous car with Hiram King driving, thus condemning me to sit in the back with Eleanor May. As with her husband, she reduced me to monosyllables. I was relieved when we reached the large and imposing grounds of Twiggleswood Court.

'Isn't it cute?' Mrs Eagleberger cried.

I well remembered the court when the Littlejohns

were there. It was furnished then, a bit untidy but homely. A family had been born and brought up in the house. Their relatives and friends came and went. There was always time for another drink, a bite and a chat about farming, horses and local gossip.

The empty court was a different place altogether. It had acquired an echo and I for one felt uneasy in it. The feeling was reinforced when we went upstairs to a rear room I had not previously seen. Jason referred to it as 'a family withdrawing room'. Tall windows looked out on, again according to Jason, 'a private garden'.

Trisha and I stood gazing down at the private garden while Jason waffled on. There was not much to see – a stretch of lawn rising to a row of trimmed yews. Beyond stood a small copse on the side of a slight rise. It was a room without a view.

As that thought came into my head I heard Mrs Eagleberger saying to Jason,

'You have not mentioned the ghost.'

'What ghost?' Jason's face went blank.

'The ghost of Miss Graham.'

'I've never heard of a ghost,' Jason declared. 'Have you?' He turned to me.

I shook my head.

'I have done my homework,' Eleanor May declared. 'I always do. I am referring to the governess. The Woman in Grey.'

I should have mentioned the American lady carried a large handbag. Out of this she produced a booklet entitled *Ghosts of the Lower Severn Valley*. It was by one Emmett Brewster and had been published privately at Mitcheldean in 1904.

'The Mitcheldean Brewsters,' Mrs Eagleberger told

us, 'are related to the West Virginian Brewsters. Is that not so Hiram?'

'Uh huh.'

'Read out,' she thrust the booklet at me, 'the marked passage on page 51.'

I turned to page 51 and read,

'There is only one ghost attributed to the remote district of Gloucestershire known as the Severnham Loop. This district contains the villages of Severnham and Twiggleswood, also the tiny hamlets of Lower Severnham and Lesser Sodham. Twiggleswood Court is one of the older buildings thereabouts. Built in the late Elizabethan era (circa 1600), it was extended during the early Victorian age.

'In the 1850s, a Miss Prudence Graham from the village of Severnham was engaged by the Twiggles family at the Court as a governess for their children. Alas Miss Graham was not prudent and allowed Sir Charles Twiggles to impregnate her. When this was discovered he sent Prudence home to her parents who then disowned her. She wandered the countryside between Twiggleswood and Severnham to die of hunger and exhaustion during the onset of winter in 1857.

'Prudence Graham used to wear a cloak with a hood made from grey West of England broadcloth. Following her death, several sightings were reported by villagers in The Loop. These were more word-of-mouth than scientifically authenticated and her apparition at Twiggleswood Court became known locally as The Woman in Grey.'

We were mentally digesting this information when Eleanor May turned to Jason and demanded of him,

'Do you believe in ghosts?'

'Well . . . ' he began.

'Don't try and avoid my question, Mr Twist. Yes or no?'

Her manner must have needled him. After all the Twists are as arrogant themselves.

'I don't believe in ghosts,' Jason answered, 'and I still wouldn't . . . even if I saw one.'

'Thought so!' Mrs Eagleberger snapped. 'Typical. What about you, Mr . . . ?' She loomed over me.

'There have been many cases recorded . . . '

'Don't hedge.'

Fortunately Trisha stepped in at this point.

'We did not know about this aspect of the property,' she said sweetly. 'Truly we did not. Are you saying a manifestation would put you off the possible purchase of Twiggleswood Court?'

'On the contrary,' Eleanor May informed us. 'I should be happy to help lay to rest the soul of poor Prudence Graham.'

Our preliminary viewing at The Court ended inconclusively. I pleaded pressure of work and made for Cheltenham. I did not learn until later that Mr Eagleberger went back to London and left the indefatigable Eleanor May at The Restoration. I also did not know what Jason and Trisha told her.

I was somewhat surprised therefore when the large American lady knocked on my cottage door at breakfast time next morning.

'Mrs Eagleberger . . . '

'That sympathetic Trisha girl told me where you lived, but forgot to give me the address of your local historian.'

'My local historian?'

'A lady who went to Oxford.'

'Ah, you mean Mrs Mead. The vicar's wife.'

'I passed the vicarage on my way here,' Mrs Eagleberger said with a trace of irritation.

'Yes, you would.'

'OK. Thank you young man for redirecting me. I shall talk to Mrs Mead on my way back.'

I thought of Dottie cooking breakfast and trying to get her children off to school. She could do without Eleanor May at this hour. On the other hand Dottie did cope better than most. There was another consideration – my nosiness. The situation intrigued me. The story could run and run.

'I'll take and introduce you to Dorothy Mead,' I heard myself saying.

As I hoped, Dottie welcomed the diversion. She eased Andy away from his book on *Classic Carburettors of the Twentieth Century* to look after the kids. She made fresh coffee and gave Mrs Eagleberger her full attention.

'I'm afraid,' said Dottie, 'Emmett Brewster's booklet is more hearsay than fact.' Eleanor May's face fell. 'But he did record local stories.' Eleanor May's face brightened. 'As a historian I can confirm the Twiggles family used to live at The Court. Equally, Grahams resided in Severnham, but moved elsewhere around the middle of the last century. In the case of Sir Charles Twiggles, he left many documents as Lord of the Manor – though none about Prudence Graham.'

'Men!' Mrs Eagleberger exclaimed. 'Typical.' At this point I left for work.

During the morning, Trisha rang to thank me for my help the previous night and I brought her up to date on Eleanor May. Trisha suggested lunch (on Jason) and I agreed.

'Silly old cow!' was how Jason described Mrs Eagleberger when we met. 'Raising a ghost at Twiggleswood Court. That's all I need.'

'We're talking about an important customer,' Trisha told him. 'One who can pull a cheque book out of that voluminous bag and sign a cheque for half a million pounds. Without feeling it. That's the sort of customer I'd kill for.'

'Well,' Jason retorted, 'you've got her.'

It transpired Eleanor May had rung them that morning and insisted on speaking to Trisha. Mrs Eagleberger was prepared to remain interested in Twiggleswood Court provided Trisha dealt with the matter and not Jason.

'What did you say?' I asked Trisha.

'I said I would be happy to help.'

'Did she mention the ghost?'

'She wanted to know my exact views. It seems those from the other side can be put off by unsympathetic characters such as Jason. She thought you were sympathetic.'

'I'm more fascinated by her and the story.'

'Good,' said Trisha, 'because I have a proposition to put to you. For a weekend together.' She gave me an irresistible smile while Jason said he had never heard so much nonsense in all his life.

'What nonsense?' I asked Trisha.

'Mrs Eagleberger wants to spend time at The Court over the weekend. Apparently Mr Eagleberger will be away on business. She feels, if two or three sympathetic people were waiting for Prudence Graham, the governess might put in an appearance. Of course I agreed and – I hope you don't mind – I suggested you.'

'All the weekend? All night perhaps?'

'No,' Trisha put me back on track. 'Just for a few hours on Saturday and maybe Sunday. But I'd very much appreciate you keeping me company in that big house.'

At this point I must make a slight diversion because it very much affects the story.

I had left London for country living and moved into my cottage at the beginning of November. Over the intervening seasons I have noticed how the weather, at that time of year, is remarkably consistent.

Living in the country makes it noticeably so. The spring sunshine, the hot summer days and a serene early autumn are suddenly replaced by the onset of winter. The weather clamps down like a shutter. Frost and fog pervade the Severn Valley. This was the period – the second weekend in November – when Mrs Eagleberger decided to keep her vigil at Twiggleswood Court and I foolishly agreed to go along with Trisha.

We met for lunch again on the Friday. Jason was not present and Trisha told me he had gone away with his wife and kids for the weekend.

'Disgusted,' she added.

'He might be wiser than us.'

'Don't be like that.'

'How do you propose to play it?'

'To start with, warm clothes. I'm putting on my thermals.'

'Passion killers.'

Trisha laughed then continued,

'Hot food and drinks. I'll organise those. Rendezvous with Mrs Eagleberger. At The Restoration. Ten a.m.'

Wearing warm old clothes I arrived at The Restoration Inn shortly before ten. It was a foggy morning and I thought about Trisha driving out from Cheltenham. Mrs

Eagleberger, in a long dark coat over a long dark dress, was pacing up and down the foyer. She greeted my 'good morning' with,

'Where's that Twist girl?'

'She has to come from Cheltenham. The fog . . . '

'Should have left earlier.'

Fortunately Trisha arrived then – carrying a holdall and wearing a multi-coloured ski suit. She started to say,

'Sorry for the slight delay. The fog . . . '

'That suit,' said Eleanor May. 'It is not conducive to raising a timid spirit.'

I nearly burst out laughing. Luckily Trisha was made of sterner stuff. In fact she was a throughgoing late twentieth-century business woman.

'You are so right, Mrs Eagleberger. I never thought . . . Thank you for bringing it to my notice. After leaving you both at Twiggleswood Court, I shall go back to Cheltenham and change into something more suitable.'

'No need,' she was told. 'I can lend you an appropriate garment.'

With that Mrs Eagleberger abruptly turned and marched up the hotel stairs. Trisha and I were left looking at each other. I wondered about the 'appropriate garment'.

The garment Eleanor May brought back with her was a huge brown and shaggy fur coat. I shall always remember the wary look Trisha gave it while still managing to smile.

'What a wonderful garment!' she cried. 'It'll keep me warm as well.'

The coat tripled Trisha's width but seemed to diminish her stature. Mrs Eagleberger buttoned it up for her, right to the top. Trisha was transformed into an awkward unkempt creature.

191

'I'll be as warm as toast,' she said between her teeth as we went out to the car park.

By the time we reached Twiggleswood Court, Trisha was red in the face. She braked the car, rather violently I thought, and seemed to fight her way out of the driver's seat.

'I'll carry the bag for you,' I said with a grin.

'Yes, do that.'

The Court on a cold foggy November morning was a different place to the friendly family home I had known. Outside, every surface was covered in water droplets. Inside, the chilling atmosphere was worsened by the echoing emptiness.

'You've chosen a ghostly sort of day,' Trisha said to Eleanor May who seemed to be sniffing the air.

'We have to find the correct spot,' Mrs Eagleberger told her, 'for the sighting.' She wandered off and we followed. We passed through the house to the back door which Trisha opened. The three of us then stood there gazing out at the fog.

'As a servant,' Eleanor May said, 'Miss Graham would come this way.'

'Surely, as governess to the children,' I suggested, 'she would have been allowed use of the front door?'

'Mrs Eagleberger is right,' Trisha agreed with her client. 'There is a definite atmosphere at the back of the house.'

'You sense it as well?' The customer was pleased.

'I do,' Trisha confirmed. 'I don't know about you, Mrs Eagleberger, but when we were here last, I particularly felt it in that back drawing room. Upstairs.'

'So did I!' Eleanor May nodded. 'We shall wait there for Miss Graham. As quiet as mice.'

With that the large lady tiptoed her way back through the house and up the stairs. She was followed by Trisha, attempting the same, though the fur coat did not help. I brought up the rear wondering what else the day would yield.

The back withdrawing room did have a chill feeling about it due, I thought, to its north-facing aspect. It was the room looking across the bare lawn to dark yews and a gloomy copse. Tendrils of fog drifted in and out of the yews like the pulling of grey threads. Mrs Eagleberger whispered,

'Yes, this is where we shall wait.'

Trisha handed me her car keys saying, 'There are three collapsible canvas chairs in my car boot. Would you get them for us? Also the rugs, kettle and camping stove.'

It took me three journeys to bring everything needed for our vigil up to the rear drawing room. By then Mrs Eagleberger and Trisha were well ensconced in their chairs with all the travel rugs wrapped round them. They suggested a hot drink so I lit the stove and made our first pot of tea.

'I usually drink coffee,' said Eleanor May, 'but this'll do I suppose.'

'Someone could go and get coffee,' Trisha glanced at me.

'No,' the customer decided. 'The stiller and the quieter we are the better. Mice-like.'

The mice-like morning proved a long one. At lunchtime I made more tea and handed round the sandwiches Trisha had brought. They contained ham and, when Mrs Eagleberger gave hers a doubtful look, I

thought for one dreadful moment she might be a
vegetarian. That was all we needed, I reflected.

The afternoon seemed even longer than the morning.
And gloomier. The fog, which had never cleared, was
thickening. Despite the hot teas and warm clothes, I felt
cold. The trouble was neither the buyer nor the seller
seemed to notice it. Apart from occasionally tiptoeing to
the toilet down the corridor, they were more intent at
staring out at the dismal scene.

'The temperature's dropping,' I ventured a remark.

'I've heard it gets noticeably colder,' Trisha whispered, 'when a manifestation is due.'

'Indeed!' breathed Mrs Eagleberger.

As it happened, I was the first to discern the Woman
in Grey. I was peering out at the ever thickening fog
when I felt the hairs on the back of my neck change into
bristles. There was someone or something between the
yews and the copse. Trisha must have seen it at the same
time for she gave a little gasp and clutched Mrs Eagleberger.

'What is it?' she whispered.

'Ssh,' Eleanor May said soothingly. 'Prudence Graham!' she called in a girlish voice. 'Prudence Graham,
come closer. We are your friends. Come closer, Prudence.'

The apparition did not stir. In fact it was difficult to
see because of the weather. Grey wisps curled round the
figure in a grey cloak. It seemed to swim in and out of
the murk.

When the Woman in Grey appeared to drift forward,
I heard Trisha whisper to Mrs Eagleberger,

'It won't come here, will it? In the house?'

'Ssh.' Eleanor May gave Trisha a pat for comfort

before again addressing the apparition. 'Prudence Graham! Prudence Graham! Come closer. Come to me. I know about you and your plight. I sympathise. I am your friend.'

However the Woman in Grey did not seem to think so. She faded into the fog and did not reappear. Her leaving left us at the window panes – rubbing them for a clearer view, opening one in vain. Mrs Eagleberger was ecstatic.

'She came! Prudence Graham knows I'm sympathetic.'

Some time elapsed before we were back to near normality. Trisha was the worst affected, shivering until I made her tea. Mrs Eagleberger remained by the window alternately gazing out and uttering words of comfort to Trisha. For my part, I could not believe what I had seen.

'Wait until I tell Jason,' Trisha still trembled as she drank the tea.

'He was an unbeliever, wasn't he?' Eleanor May did not turn her head.

'He says – if there is the merest hint of a ghost – the property will never sell.'

'Well, he is going to be proved wrong a second time,' Mrs Eagleberger retorted. 'I saw Miss Graham – the poor lost soul – with my own eyes. Prudence has been drawn to me. When this cold empty house becomes a warm welcoming home, perhaps she will venture nearer. You cannot dictate to the spirits,' she sternly informed me.

'No, I suppose not.'

By then Trisha was sufficiently recovered to have me move everything back to the car while allowing Eleanor May to go on comforting her. We travelled to The

Restoration where, in the lounge annexe, the Severnham Ladies Club were having tea. As it was tea time, the waitress asked if we would like to order the same. Trisha, who was back to her usual self, remembered her client preferred coffee.

People often ask me 'What happened afterwards?' It is a good question because, in all too many cases, the end results are far different from first intentions.

In the case of Mrs Eagleberger, she purchased Twiggleswood Court and lived there for a couple of years before appearing to lose interest. The Twists then – in the complicated ways they love to follow – did some sort of leaseback deal. The property was occupied from time to time by people from the US Embassy. This happens more than we realise in the Cotswolds and in the Severn Valley. Americans, Arabs, Germans and Japanese like to pay us compliments by occupying our loveliest places.

Trisha did not remain long at the Cheltenham office. She returned to London where the money is. When I met her again in later years, Trisha had become brittle and hard.

Last but not least, Jason brought me a case of wine soon after the ghost-hunting incident.

'For your help,' he said. As he was closing the car boot I glimpsed a rolled-up grey garment.

Happy Christmas

As with all good feuds, the one between Colin Fluke and
Arnold Barter simmered for a long time before coming
to the boil. Let me begin by introducing the two
contestants.

Colin belonged to the new generation of Flukes who
were determined to make their own way in life despite
circumstances and the Twists being against them. He did
well at school and passed exams which led him to trade
training. Colin decided to be a plumber, served an
apprenticeship then started to build up his own business.

Physically he reflected capability. An affable yet serious young man, he worked hard and talked straight.

Since childhood Colin had gone out with Sally Hopskip, granddaughter of my neighbours. She trained to be a nurse and, after a stint in Cheltenham Hospital, joined our Dr Prosser at Severnham Health Centre. Colin and Sally were quietly married and set up home in a bungalow at the Fluke end of the village.

Now for Arnold Barter. He was a newcomer. His bank had a sub-branch in Severnham and he arrived to be its manager. As the village grew, Arnold did the same – expanding the premises and taking on more staff. He was a big smiling man of the type Elizabeth Spinks described as 'over-friendly'. His female staff said they did not like being alone in the same room as him though nothing amiss was ever reported.

Arnold married a Martha Scholey from Stroud. It was said by the villagers that she 'had the money'. How they found out such facts would always remain a mystery to me, but they were usually right. Martha had a broker brother in Gloucester and played the Stock Exchange. When our Chief Councillor Conrad Twist built his ten prestigious houses on Severnham Hill, the Barters immediately sought and bought No. 3.

When did the feud start between these two dissimilar local characters? Many people claimed it was because Colin wanted an extra large loan to further his plumbing business. That took place around the same time, but I believe the first sign of mutual antipathy occurred in full public view at a village cricket match.

Cricket is not all white flannels and lazy afternoons on the village green. It is deceptive and can be a sneaky game. I never thought village relationships were helped by Conrad Twist instigating an annual Gentlemen versus Players match. He considered himself a classic batsman and of course a captain by nature. This game in early June served to reinforce a division between the Severnham haves and the have-nots – between Twists and their friends against Flukes and the rest.

Andy Mead our vicar, Edward Spinks the grocer and I often joined other teams, but we kept out of the Gentlemen versus Players match. Nevertheless it was a village occasion with scrumptious teas laid on by the Severnham ladies.

I am not going to describe the whole match where, to my mind, the feud started. Suffice to say Conrad Twist won the toss for the Gentlemen and decided to go in first. Naturally he would be the opening batsman and Arnold Barter was honoured as his partner. Both men looked splendid when they strode out of the pavilion acknowledging applause.

Colin Fluke opened the bowling for the Players. He was not an outstanding bowler, but his consistency and accuracy made up for this. Colin could bowl to every length and hit any of the three stumps. Conrad blocked the initial four balls of the over and scored a single with the fifth. This left Arnold facing Colin who cleaned bowled him on the sixth delivery.

'Oh ahs,' rippled round the Players as Arnold Barter made his way back to the pavilion. The situation was not helped by Basher Fluke calling to Colin,

'You won't be getting that bank loan then.'

All present knew Colin was hoping to expand his plumbing business, but needed more capital.

At the time Colin Fluke did his work from a beaten-up old white van filled with borrowed tools. He carried few spares, which meant journeys into Cheltenham or Gloucester during most jobs. The business plan Edward

Spinks had helped Colin to produce included purchasing a new and larger van with radio telephone, more plumbing tools, plus fitting out a shed behind Colin's bungalow to store spares.

We heard there was some hilarity in the bank when Colin entered clutching his business plan. Most of the village knew what he was after. Janis Palmer was there and she is always keen on a good laugh.

'You'll never get it, Colin,' Janis called, 'after bowling out Mr Barter.'

'Oh ah.' Other Severnham customers were heard to say.

Then Arnold Barter appeared at his office door and asked Colin to 'come on in'.

I was talking to Edward Spinks by the barn he used as a store for grocery supplies when Colin arrived grinning.

'You've got it?' Edward greeted him.

'Oh ah.' Colin waved an envelope.

'Congratulations!' we both said.

'I've to watch me cash flow mind.'

'We all have.'

'I'm very grateful to you, Mr Spinks.'

'You're going to be more grateful,' said Edward, 'because your first job could be here. This barn has always been damp and, as you know, I have had a new floor laid. I'd like a boiler in one corner and some radiators round the sides. Could you manage that, Colin?'

'Like you said Mr Spinks, it'll be my first job.'

'When you finish it,' I said, 'come and see me. My cottage could do with some central heating.'

So Colin Fluke bought a new white van, a set of plumber's tools and all the necessary spares. He fitted out the interiors of the van and his shed with everything in its correct place. After ten days work at Edward's barn, Colin came to me.

'Here I am,' he said. 'Like I promised.'

'That's great.'

We moved around the cottage talking about central heating boilers, radiators and pipe runs.

'You realise,' Colin warned me, 'there'll be a bit of an upheaval like?'

'Yes. You have to drill through some solid walls.'

'I'll clear up as I go.'

'I'm sure you will, Colin.'

Once we had agreed on what was to be done – and the price – I left him to it. Each evening, on returning from work, I could see the progress Colin had made. By the end of the week, my central heating was installed and working.

Both Edward Spinks and I paid immediately to give Colin's cash flow a fair start. I asked him if he had other jobs lined up and a work diary was produced. He said,

'I'm at the Health Centre next week. Sally arranged that. Then I've got a couple of jobs on the Meadowsweet Estate. I keep putting me cards through doors and people ring up.'

'That's marvellous, Colin!'

'Sally and me are ever so pleased.'

Colin's business proved brisk for the initial six months. Although he paid in what he could to the bank and Sally did the same out of her wages the overdraft did not go down. Their first Christmas came and went. Despite a fairly hard January and February, with burst pipes and resultant plumbing problems, business was slack. Other plumbers and tradespeople said the same.

Although ministers stated no recession was even in sight, the rest of the country knew otherwise.

There was clearly a limit to the number of plumbing and central heating jobs in and around Severnham. Therefore Colin began to look further afield. He started travelling one day, then two or three days a week to Cheltenham, Gloucester and Tewkesbury in search of work – often passing other plumbers from those places trying Severnham. It was a difficult spring for him and he lost a lot of weight.

His cousin Chris Fluke – of the electronic success story – had warned Colin never, but never, to do a job for Tiny Palmer. On the other hand Tiny, who knew Colin was looking for work, kept greeting him with,

'When are you going to come and do that big job of mine?'

The big job meant a considerable amount of plumbing at a new milking shed for Tiny Palmer's prize Jersey herd. In the end Colin went, costed it out and asked for half in advance.

'You're joking,' said Tiny. Eventually, to keep working, Colin made a start.

This turned out to be a typical Palmer job. Tiny either found one fault after another or called for additions which he later denied.

'Oh come off it, Colin. I never asked you to do all that.'

Colin tried making notes with dates and times whenever Tiny wanted more, but the cheerful open-faced customer was on to the next thing. Janis Palmer was equally cheerful as if nothing was amiss. The milking shed job went on long after its allotted span.

Then came the bill, which Tiny queried. And the

statement, which Tiny lost. Meanwhile Colin's cash flow was in a sorry state and Mr Barter requested a meeting. At the showdown, according to Edward, the bank manager said that – on forward projections – Colin could not continue for many more months.

'Oh dear!' Edward commiserated when he heard the sorry story. 'What are you going to do?'

'I have to find more work. Luckily Mr Barter thought he could help me . . . '

'Arnold Barter help you?'

'There's quite a big job at his place.'

'What is it, Colin? If I may ask.'

'Don't know yet. Something to do with Mrs Barter. Have to go and see her.'

'Well,' Edward said doubtfully, 'I wish you the best of luck.'

Up to then not much was known about Martha Barter apart from her being the bank manager's wife, the one with the money and a 'Stroudie'. The latter meant she was almost a foreigner – coming from twenty miles away. According to the Severnham folk, 'them Stroudies' were different and difficult. As were people in the nearby Forest of Dean, on the Cotswold Hills; in fact all those outside the Severn Valley.

I learned what was happening at the Barter's house from Colin's wife Sally when she came to visit her grandparents. Sally was a stocky resolute little woman. I saw her picking flowers and she called out to me across the fence.

'I'm terrible!' she cried. 'Always raiding their garden every time I come here.'

'I'm sure they want you to,' I said. 'How's Colin?'

A shadow passed over Sally's face.

'Not very happy.'

'Why is that?'

'The job up at the Barters.'

'Oh?'

'It's awkward like. You know Conrad Twist had them houses built – one for himself and the others for his rich acquaintances. Always ties things up tight, does our Chief Councillor. Before anyone could purchase, they had to agree to certain conditions. The first was they were not allowed to make major alterations without consulting him.'

'How is Colin affected?'

'Well, while Conrad Twist discusses proposed alterations with his neighbours, he talks them into using his own building firm. Some services, such as plumbing and central heating, are sub-contracted. In this case, Arnold Barter asked for Colin.'

'That's good . . . '

'Not really. It's the set-up.'

'In what way?'

'The main contractors are Twists. The sub-contractor a Fluke, you see.'

'Yes, I do see.'

'Colin doesn't get much co-operation from them. There's also her.'

'Who?'

'Martha Barter. The Stroudie.'

It took a while to obtain the foregoing information so I shall give the rest of it straight.

The extension to No. 3 Upper Severnham Lane was for Mrs Barter to have her own office. She had made money playing the Stock Exchange and the office was intended to make more money. It would be linked by a system of computers, telephones and faxes – not only to her broker brother in Gloucester – but also direct to the major temples of Mammon.

All this necessitated a larger and more expensive boiler for the house as well as a finely tuned control system. In turn that demanded close co-operation between builder and plumber – a condition which no Twist would give a Fluke. The situation worried Edward Spinks.

'The Barters,' he told me when delivering my groceries, 'are running Colin into the ground. Arnold about the overdraft. Martha with the new system.'

I would see Colin Fluke's van go past my cottage early in the mornings and return late in the evenings. He would be up there on Severnham Hill during the weekends. Suddenly there was no sign of him.

'I haven't seen Colin this last week,' I remarked to Edward, who replied,

'No, you wouldn't.'

'Why not?'

'He's gone bust.'

'Never!'

'I'm afraid so.'

'What happened?'

'He went over the top moneywise – because of Martha's requirements – then Arnold called in the overdraft.'

'Can he do that?'

'Arnold did. It's the talk of the village. I wonder you hadn't heard. There's worse. Bailiffs came from Gloucester to take away Colin's van, tools and strip the bungalow bare. The rest of the Flukes are up in arms.'

Colin's business troubles and Mrs Eagleberger's ghost

hunting took place around the same time. By then November had changed to December and the run-up to our Christmas commenced.

Christmas in Severnham is much the same as else-where, but ours is a little more do-it-yourself I think. I have told about the children's Christmas pantomime in the story of Sandy Porridge. His place was taken by another character from the actors' home at Cradley Heath and the production this year was *Aladdin*. Christmas decorations appeared throughout the village and various social activities were being busily organised.

I placed a small Christmas tree in the front downstairs window of my cottage. The Hopskips next door strung coloured lights round their backyard. At the church, the good ladies of Severnham festooned every surface with holly and ivy. Dottie Mead decorated the old vicarage in Victorian style while Spinks Stores had a most fabulous display including a Father Christmas grotto and free toys for the under-fives. A 20-foot fir outside the council offices was clearly labelled 'The Twist Tree'.

In the case of our two inns – The Boar's Head or Piggy sported flashing lights and extra kegs for what had become infamous as the Fluke's Big Bash on Christmas Eve. As for The Restoration Inn, Polly carefully super-vised its decorations. There would be a series of parties, of which the most notable this year was a visit by the Gloucestershire Constabulary, also on Christmas Eve.

The Restoration often had police parties during the year. It was a handy place for the officers to let their hair down metaphorically speaking. In the case of the Christmas Eve party this was an event for which our chief councillor Conrad Twist had fought long and hard. Conrad often mentioned how he and the chief constable

206

were 'just like that'. At last he managed to have a party for them at Severnham. This would be attended by what he called 'the top officers and my personal guests.'

'The fuss!' Polly said. 'He's driving me scatty. Every day there are changes and new arrangements. It started with a small reception. Then it became a full scale dinner. Now there's to be dancing. He tells me dancing is called a gig nowadays. Plenty of booze, he keeps stressing. Are they going to drink and drive, I ventured to ask. He was furious at my question. They are the police, he snapped. Who's to arrest them?'

Conrad Twist had the annoying habit of considering his event to be all important. Poor Polly was inundated by commands and counter-commands from the council offices. The guest list grew, was altered, cancelled and reissued as the days went by. In this welter of preparations, two items interested the rest of us. First there was Conrad Twist's top table. It of course included him and Hilda, the poor chief constable and his wife, also the Barters – Arnold and Martha – among others. Secondly there were the extra hands taken on by Polly to serve the police guests. Their ranks contained Colin Fluke.

I should mention Colin had not reached the breadline. His wife Sally was still employed at the Health Centre, while Colin was doing odd plumbing and any other kind of job going to bring in the money. True friends put what work they could his way. It was also known the Flukes were still furious at how their Colin had been treated by Arnold Barter the bank manager. Dire warnings were made.

'Something is going to happen,' Edward Spinks said to me. 'In the old days they would simply have waylaid and beaten up our Arnold. Nowadays they're more subtle.'

What happened was so subtle and complex, I have to unravel the story and rearrange it in a meaningful sequence. The reader should realise the many activities taking place in and around Severnham on this Christmas Eve. At The Restoration there was the police party. At The Piggy there were the Flukes supposedly celebrating. The rest of us in the village went about our various activities. Let me begin with the dinner dance.

Polly did her best as usual. Conrad Twist and his personal guests, in dinner jackets and evening gowns, sat at the top table. The other tables were occupied by beefy officers with their wives and girl friends. Many officers wore plain suits, but by mutual consent the ladies remained resplendent. At the far (lower) end of the dining room, our PC Stan Oakshott supped a quiet pint with one or two of the boys. He and they were on duty. After all it was Christmas Eve.

By all accounts Colin Fluke kept to the lower end of the dining room. However, as he happened to pass the top table, Conrad Twist beckoned him.

'Yes, Mr Twist?' Colin was all attention and civil.

'Mr Barter here would like a word with you.'

'Yes, Mr Barter?' Colin remained civil.

'Keeping busy I see?' said the bank manager.

'Yes Sir. Is there anything else?'

'No. Not really, Colin. Just wanted to wish you a Happy Christmas.'

'The same to you, Sir. A Happy Christmas.'

Many people witnessed this exchange and later everyone confirmed it was cool but innocuous.

Dinner at The Restoration went on until well after

ten, when the company moved into the cleared lounge for dancing and further drinking. Colin continued to serve drinks, together with the rest of the inn staff, but PC Oakshott slipped away. Stan walked down the High Street as far as The Piggy where the Flukes insisted he shared a pint of best ale with them.

I mention these minor details because, as in the best of detective yarns, they are vital to the main plot.

At half-past eleven, the majority of what one might call the village centre party began to converge on the church for Midnight Mass. There was a goodly number, including children to give their much rehearsed rendering of 'Away in a Manger'.

When we emerged uplifted, it was to see a high frosty sky in which the stars twinkled like sparklers. People called their 'Happy Christmas' greetings, shook each other by the hand and exchanged not a few kisses. PC Oakshott was present, standing to one side, still on duty and looking somewhat formal. As I approached him, so did the Spinks.

'Happy Christmas, Stan!' said Edward. 'No crime wave, I hope?'

'Now why would you be saying that?' Stan enquired.

'Just my silly attempt at a stupid joke,' Edward apologised with a frown at me. Soon afterwards, when Stan had departed, Edward asked, 'What's got into him?' I shrugged.

We went to our respective homes, but Stan returned to The Restoration where the police party was coming to an end. He arrived just as Conrad Twist was trying to persuade the chief constable to 'pop up my place on the hill for a nightcap'.

'Love to,' came the reply, 'but I've kept my driver far too long already.'

Once the chief constable had departed, most of the other policemen and their ladies left as well. By then Polly and the staff were beginning to clear away. Stan wandered through the hotel into the kitchen and saw Colin Fluke was still there.

'A long night,' Stan said to Colin.

'Not if you're being paid by the hour,' Colin replied.

'I think I'll look in again at The Piggy,' Stan told him.

Oakshott of the Yard once more walked down Severnham's High Street to The Boar's Head. There he saw a few Flukes headed by Garnet having last drinks in front of a dying fire. Dai Williams the proprietor had joined them while Gwen, a noted cook, was putting the finishing touches to the Christmas turkey in the kitchen behind the bar.

'Why it's Stan again!' Basher greeted Oakshott.

'Can't you sleep?' asked Charlie.

Dai offered our constable another pint of best ale, but Stan only had a half then said he best be getting home. He did so and found his Jackie with her sister Janis having one of their laughs together. At that moment the phone rang.

'Oakshott,' came Conrad Twist's voice. 'I want you up here right away.' The line went dead.

For some reason known only to him, Stan decided not to use his car, but to go by bike. It would give him time, he explained 'to blow out the cobwebs' – a remark which made the sisters laugh all the more. I heard this from Elizabeth Spinks days later and include it here to maintain the sequence.

So Stan got out his bike, checked the lights were

210

working, put on his clips and pedalled along the lane
past my cottage. I saw him as I was opening the
bedroom window and shouted,

'Happy Christmas, Stan!'

'Happy Christmas!' he called back. I watched the red
tail light turn into Upper Severnham Lane and wondered.

When Stan reached No. 1 Upper Severnham Lane, he
propped his bike against the gatepost, went to the front
door and rang the bell. The door was opened by Hilda
Twist who, Stan said later, 'had one of them big round
brandy glasses in her hand'. He greeted her with,

'Happy Christmas morning, Mrs Twist. What is the
trouble?'

'No. 3,' she replied.

'Mr Twist asked me to come here.'

'He's at No. 3.'

'I see. Sorry to have bothered you.' Stan turned to go.
It was then he saw Mrs Barter standing behind Mrs
Twist. Martha, like Hilda, held a brandy glass.

'I thought,' Stan said again later, 'they were both
pissed or something. Mrs Barter looked disapproving
like. Sort of dark faced. You can never tell with them
Stroudies.'

Anyway Oakshott of the Yard left No. 1 and went to
No. 3. There the front door was opened by Conrad Twist
with Arnold Barter standing beside him. Both men held
tumblers of whisky.

'You took your time getting here,' Conrad barked at
Stan.

'Happy Christmas morning, Sir . . . ' Stan started to
say.

'Come in man. There's enough cold in the house already.'

Stan stepped into the hall of No. 3 and waited. From his experience of Chief Councillor Twist, the reason for the summons would be stated sooner rather than later. Conrad said,

'You're going to have . . . to arrest Colin Fluke.'

It transpired the Barters had returned from the dance to the Twists for final drinks. Arnold and Martha then left and went to their own home. On opening the front door Martha remarked how cold the house was. Had Arnold altered the central heating boiler? He certainly had not. Well he should go and see what was wrong. He would.

'Arnold rang me,' Conrad Twist patiently explained to Stan Oakshott, 'and I came right over. This way.' He led Oakshott through the house and outside to the boiler room. It stood behind the recent extension – a big fuel oil tank by a small separate structure. Twist opened the boiler room door.

'Was the door locked as part of your security system?' Stan asked Arnold.

'No,' the bank manager admitted, 'we thought . . . '

'Come along, Stan!' Conrad put on the light.

Oakshott of the Yard soon saw what was the matter. The boiler had gone. All that remained in the room were ends of pipes and water on the floor.

'At least Colin Fluke turned off the fuel tap,' Conrad said, 'or you could have had him for arson as well.'

'As well as what, Sir?'

'Theft!' Conrad Twist shouted. 'Do I have to spell it out for you?'

'No, Sir. I understand your line of thinking, but Colin

Fluke spent the entire evening serving drinks. As you know.'

Arnold Barter took over the conversation at this stage.

'Constable,' he reasoned, 'it can only be Colin Twist. He installed the boiler. He knew the boiler room was not part of the house security system.'

'I understand Sir,' Stan carefully chose his words, 'no payment was made for work done or the article in question?'

'His business failed . . . ' Barter began.

'We're not talking about some fiddling little business,' Conrad Twist shouted angrily. 'We're talking about theft and but for the grace of God – arson! The blaze could have spread to envelop all of us.'

Later Stan told me about the rest of his Christmas night or rather the beginning of Christmas morning. He made a start by getting away from the Barters and the Twists to phone HQ. Headquarters were unsympathetic. They were short staffed. They were not coming out to Severnham again. Stan would just have to deal with the stupid situation there himself.

So Stan went and knocked up Colin Fluke. As expected Colin knew nothing. He had worked from before six to after midnight. Dozens of people saw him as well as Stan, Conrad Twist and Mr Bloody Barter. Colin stressed he had not done anything.

'If you didn't do it, Colin,' Stan said, 'some of your other Flukes did.'

'Well no one told me. Leave over, Stan. It's Christmas morning and I'm knackered.'

The nest of Flukes extended well beyond the lower village. It consisted of half houses and small bungalows, decrepit barns and tin sheds, much divided and subdivided by chicken wire, chestnut fencing and the like. As Stan wandered around, noting the various clapped out lorries and aged fishing boats, he knew exactly how the deed had been done.

First would come mutterings at The Boar's Head. Next, if there was to be any action, Garnet would nod to the Flukes concerned. Oakshott of the Yard could just see the operation. Three or four Flukes would slip along to Upper Severnham Lane while Arnold Barter enjoyed himself and Colin worked. The boiler would then be taken to the river and dumped. If Stan searched long enough he might find a warmish lorry engine or a dampish boat. But doing so would muck up everyone's Christmas. And, in the end, could he prove it?

This story has an interesting sequel. Edward Spinks was so disgusted by the way Arnold Barter had acted, he wrote to the bank chairman who was an old City friend. The chairman replied some time later to say his people had investigated the matter and, it would seem, Mr Barter looked after the best interests of the bank. In view of this Barter was being promoted – meaning moved sideways – to their Pershore branch. Arnold commuted there by car each day because Martha preferred to remain in her present home. This state of affairs continued until . . . but that is yet another Severnham story.

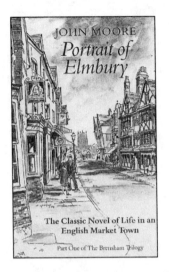

The first book of the famous trilogy of English country life, *The Brensham Trilogy*, by John Moore. Fifty years after its first publication in 1945, it is republished for today's readers in a new paperback edition from The Windrush Press.

TO ORDER: Please send a cheque, payable to The Windrush Press, for £6.99 to Orders Dept, The Windrush Press, Little Window, High Street, Moreton-in-Marsh, Glos GL56 0LL (Tel: 01608 652025) with your name and delivery address.

✂ ···

ORDER FORM
I enclose a cheque payable to THE WINDRUSH PRESS for £ ....
(£6.99 for each book).
Please send me (quantity) .... copies of
PORTRAIT OF ELMBURY to the following address:

....

....

Name: ....

Tel No: ....

If you have enjoyed this book, now read the first title *Cottage in the Country* also about the village of Severnham and its inhabitants.

TO ORDER: Please send a cheque, payable to The Windrush Press, for £6.99 to Orders Dept, The Windrush Press, Little Window, High Street, Moreton-in-Marsh, Glos GL56 0LL (Tel: 01608 652025) with your name and delivery address.

✂ ....

ORDER FORM
I enclose a cheque payable to THE WINDRUSH PRESS for £ ....
(£6.99 for each book).
Please send me (quantity) .... copies of
COTTAGE IN THE COUNTRY to the following address:

....
....
Name: ....
Tel No:..